SEALED WITH TRUST

A CHRISTIAN K9 ROMANTIC SUSPENSE

LAURA SCOTT

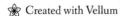

CHAPTER ONE

"What time are you coming home?" Laney asked.

"Soon, sweetie." Maggie Chandler smiled as she spoke to her eight-year-old daughter using the hands-free function in her police-issued SUV. "Tell Nanna I'll be home for dinner, okay?"

"We're having spaghetti and meatballs!" Laney's voice rose with excitement. "My favorite."

"Yum," Maggie agreed, shaking her head wryly. Her mother would do anything to make Laney happy. Maggie was blessed to have her mother's help in watching her daughter while she was at work. "See you soon."

"Okay, bye." Laney disconnected from the call.

Maggie's smile faded when she noticed several buzzards dropping from the sky to land on a particular area in the dry, hot central Texas landscape. Likely a dead animal, but her cop instincts jangled enough that she slowed her speed and took the SUV off-road toward the flock of birds. At nearly four o'clock in the afternoon, the sun was still high enough to make it difficult to see, even with her sunglasses.

As she grew closer, she saw a lumpy shape lying on the ground. It was bigger than a coyote but smaller than a cow. Too wide to be a deer. Not long enough to be a horse. The birds flew back up into the sky as she approached, but they continued to circle up above, waiting patiently for her to leave so they could get back to their feast.

Two minutes later, she swallowed hard when she recognized the lumpy shape wasn't an animal, but a human. Based on the buzzards, she felt certain the person was dead, but she knew she needed to be sure. Quickly hitting the brake, she threw the vehicle into park and killed the engine. When she stepped out into the stifling August heat, the acrid scent told her everything she needed to know.

The person was dead and had been for at least a few hours. Probably longer.

The August heat was oppressive as usual, and she instantly began to sweat despite her short-sleeved blue blouse and thin dress slacks. As one of three detectives for the criminal investigative unit of the Fredericksburg Police Department, this wasn't her first dead body. But crime in this small, quaint tourist town was generally related to sexual assaults, drugs, and alcohol abuse.

Not murder.

Granted, she knew better than to assume foul play. It was possible this victim had gotten drunk and died out here of natural causes, but that scenario wasn't likely. For one thing, she was in the middle of Highway 16, not anywhere near any bars or taverns. There also wasn't a vehicle nearby. How had the victim gotten here? Walked? Or had the victim been dropped off by a friend or rideshare? She swept her gaze over the area, her investigative mind spinning with various possibilities.

Moving cautiously as to not disturb the crime scene, she edged closer. The hard, dry ground didn't reveal footprints that she could see.

It only took a moment to identify the body as male, lying partially on his side. She angled around toward the feet to get a better look. Then abruptly reared back when she recognized the victim as Tate Chandler, her ex-husband. His face had already been pecked at by the birds, but there was no mistaking his bright red hair, his beard, and his bicep tattoo where he'd inked her name. *Maggie.*

There was also a bullet hole in the center of his forehead.

Covering her hand with her mouth, she turned and hurried back to the SUV. She needed to call this in. She fumbled with her phone, feeling like a rookie patrol officer on her first day.

"Dispatch, this is Detective Chandler. I'm ten miles outside of town on Highway 16 and found a body. Victim appears to be former Fredericksburg police officer Tate Chandler."

"Your husband?" Dispatcher Delilah Hall asked, her voice high and squeaky.

"Ex-husband." She leaned weakly against her SUV, wishing she could erase the image of Tate's dead face from her mind. "And you need to let Lieutenant Fernando know because there's a bullet hole in the center of his forehead and no gun lying nearby to indicate it was self-inflicted. I have no doubt this is a homicide."

Delilah audibly gasped. "You can't work the case, Maggie, that's a conflict of interest. I'll call Simmons."

She knew that was true, the vic being her ex was absolutely a conflict of interest. Yet their police department was very small, so she doubted she'd be able to avoid participating in the investigation. Maybe they'd give her the menial tasks to do. "Let Fernando know I'll be here waiting for the rest of the team."

"Will do."

Maggie pocketed her phone, feeling sick at seeing her ex-husband's dead body. She and Tate had been divorced for four years now, and he'd recently started causing trouble again over their custody arrangement. After being mostly nonexistent in Laney's life over the past four years, suddenly he wanted to pick up where he'd left off before their divorce. As if Laney was still the four-year-old who'd fawned over him, rather than the cheeky eight-year-old who rarely asked about her father. Deep down, it irritated her because Tate knew the truth and was simply using Laney as a pawn in his war against her. But knowing that didn't change the situation, so she'd been forced to call her lawyer to deal with his latest threat. Tate's plan was to have Laney stay with him in Austin during the entire school year where the academics were allegedly so much better than what Fredericksburg had to offer. Oh, and his schedule was so much better than hers, too, with fewer call hours. She'd tried to point out that Laney had friends here and that she barely knew her father anymore, but Tate had insisted he was only doing what was best for their daughter.

Yeah, right. After barely seeing her except at Christmas and two weeks during the summer, even that being two years ago? Not.

Their last conversation played over in her mind. Like she was the bad mother who didn't care about Laney's education and well-being instead of the other way around.

Now he was dead. Murdered. Who would do such a thing? And why?

She turned back to look at the scene, again wondering why his body had been left all the way out here in the middle of nowhere. A couple of brave buzzards had dropped back down to the body.

"Hiya! Go away!" She waved her arms and jumped up and down to shoo them off. A little like closing the barn door after the horses escaped, but she couldn't stand the idea of them going after Tate's dead body.

She didn't love him, which had been the real reason their marriage hadn't lasted. But she had cared about him. At least in the beginning.

Her mind was still reeling when Lieutenant Antonio Fernando arrived, followed shortly thereafter by senior detective, Kent Simmons. Both men looked grim as they approached.

"Maggie." Fernando greeted her with a nod. "What happened?"

"I was making my last round through the area. I happened to notice the buzzards circling overhead and came over to investigate." She gestured toward the scene to their right. "I only went close enough to recognize the dead victim as Tate and that he'd been murdered. I didn't touch anything at the crime scene."

The lieutenant exchanged a concerned glance with Kent Simmons. "Okay, stay here. We'll check it out."

Hanging back wasn't easy. Despite being the youngest detective on their small team and a woman, she was usually treated fairly. Simmons, who was ten years her senior, often worked cases with her, under Fernando's tutelage.

But not this time, she realized grimly. No, this time she'd be kept out of the information loop. At least initially while Simmons retraced Tate's last movements.

She thought about their angry conversation just last

night. About how she'd accused him of retaliating against her for the divorce by attacking their joint custody agreement. After all, he was the one who'd quit the Fredericksburg police force. He was the one who'd relocated ninety miles away to Austin for his new job working private security for some rich guy. He was the one who'd always had a reason he couldn't come visit or have her drop Laney to Austin per the co-custody agreement. Now he was sending her legal paperwork to challenge their agreement? She'd pretty much told him that would only happen over her dead body.

Now *he* was dead.

A chill snaked over her despite the hot sun. She abruptly frowned. Had Tate been in Austin last night when he'd called? Or had he been here in Fredericksburg? That he was here now made her think the latter. Her first thought was to get his phone records, to track his calls and where he'd been, then she remembered it wasn't her case.

Blowing out a long breath, she watched as the lieutenant and Simmons walked around the body, taking photos with their phones and speaking in hushed tones. Turning toward the highway, she could see the boxy shape of the forensic van heading toward the scene. It would take a while to search for evidence, especially since small animals could have carried some away. Would they let her help search? Or would they send her straight home?

Belatedly, she winced, thinking of the conversation she'd need to have with Laney. The little girl had lost the only father figure she'd ever known. Telling Laney she'd never see her father again would be heartbreaking.

The only bright side was that Laney rarely asked about her dad. His being in Austin had created a rift between them. No bad feelings, just more of an out-of-sight, out-of-mind scenario.

Maybe it is my fault, Maggie thought wearily. Maybe she should have tried harder to make things work. She could have considered moving to Austin; most police departments were hiring these days. But she hadn't wanted to give up her position here in Fredericksburg. Simmons had spoken of retiring in a few years, had even put money down on a nice property near the ocean in Corpus Christi. His leaving would make her the senior detective.

Had her selfishness contributed to Tate's death?

As soon as the thought entered her mind, she shook it off. Her not moving to Austin hadn't put the bullet hole in Tate's forehead. A person had done that. But who? And why?

"Maggie?" Lieutenant Fernando's voice interrupted her thoughts.

"Yes?" She turned to face him. Her boss was striding toward her with an enigmatic expression on his face. "Did you find something?"

He hesitated. "No, but I'd like to ask you a few questions."

"Sure, although I'm not sure how much I can help."

"When did you last see or hear from your ex-husband?"

"I haven't seen him in well over two years, but I spoke to him last night. He got some crazy idea to challenge the custody agreement despite not seeing Laney as often as he was scheduled to in the first place."

"You argued?" Fernando asked.

Her instincts went on high alert, and she wished she'd chosen her words more carefully. Having an argument with a man who'd recently been murdered made her look like a suspect. "We had a conversation," she said, backpedaling. "I told him our lawyers would need to be involved if he wanted to change the agreement."

"That means fighting it out in court, right?" Fernando asked.

Her cheeks flushed, and beads of sweat rolled down from her temples, not just because of the one-hundred-degree temps. She didn't like sitting on the hot seat like some perp. "To be honest, I didn't think he was serious about the proposal. Like I said, he rarely took Laney on the weekends he was supposed to. So why would he suddenly want an eight-year-old child running around full time? It didn't make any sense."

Fernando didn't say anything for a long moment, waiting for her to continue. It was a technique detectives used with suspects. Interesting how difficult it was to stay silent when you wanted nothing more than to loudly and earnestly proclaim your innocence.

Somehow, she managed to hold her tongue. The forensic van had arrived, Jackie the tech going to work.

"Look, I can help collect evidence—"

"No, you can't." Fernando cut her off midsentence. "You need to give me your gun and your shield and head home."

She stared at him. "Why are you taking my gun and shield?"

"You know why." Fernando held out his hand impatiently. "You're too close to this, and we need to clear you before I can let you come back to work."

Clear her? It took a moment for the realization to sink in. "You can't seriously believe I'm a suspect? Come on, Loo, I was home all night and worked my shift all day. Besides, I would never do something like this."

Fernando waved his fingers. "Shield and gun."

Feeling as if she'd walked into some sort of horror show, Maggie removed her badge and gun from her belt holster. After dropping them into his outstretched hand, she turned and yanked the driver's side door of her SUV open.

Simmons had joined Fernando. No one said a word as she slid behind the wheel, started the engine, cranked the air-conditioning, and backed away from the crime scene.

She drove in a daze, hardly able to comprehend what had just happened. She'd found her ex-husband's dead body lying in the middle of nowhere and was now a suspect in his murder.

The worst part of all? The small wave of relief that washed over her at knowing Laney's custody arrangement wouldn't change. A man had lost his life, had been deliberately shot in the head. It was wrong to be relieved.

Yet marrying Tate had been a mistake. One she'd done to cover another lapse in judgment. At the time, she'd thought marrying Tate was the right thing to do, for Laney's sake.

She'd been wrong.

As she drove to her mother's house, she couldn't help but wonder if this was God's way of punishing her for her sins. And while she may deserve God's penance, Laney didn't.

Her daughter was the true innocent in this.

RETIRED former Navy SEAL Dallas Hoffman glanced at his chocolate lab, Romeo, via the rearview mirror. Romeo looked content despite the way the poor canine had been cooped up longer than usual. "We'll be there soon, boy," he said.

Romeo thumped his tail in response.

His sister, Brenda, called him constantly for help. She ran a small tourist store in downtown Fredericksburg, and her latest proposition was that she wanted him to be her private, unpaid security guard to prevent shoplifting. Apparently, some of the teenagers thought it was a game to steal stuff they didn't even want just to prove they could get away with it. Brenda's son, Jason, was one of the perpetrators. Since Brenda's divorce, Jason had been acting out. This was just one of the latest examples.

Dallas loved his sister and cared about his nephew, so he always came when she called. Yet he couldn't help feeling frustrated. Her crisis situations were nothing compared to what he'd dealt with during his twenty-year stint as a Navy SEAL.

He instinctively rubbed his sore left shoulder. The one that had been reconstructed back in January after their last op had gone sideways. He and his five teammates—Mason, Kaleb, Hudd, Dawson, and Nico—had been lucky to survive, but Jaydon hadn't. Their extraction had been dicey, tangos shooting hot on their heels as they hit the water to head for the ship waiting for them. They'd never anticipated an underwater bomb.

Until the explosion had sent them spinning and tumbling through the water.

His taking shrapnel in the shoulder and Kaleb Tyson's blown-out knee had been the least damaging of the assault. Senior Chief Mason Gray had lost his hearing in one ear and suffered a partial loss of hearing in the other, Hudd Foster had lost vision in one eye and suffered debilitating headaches, Dawson Steele had taken a belly load of shrapnel that had resulted in four separate surgeries, and Nico Ramirez ruptured his Achilles tendon. Nico was also Jaydon's swim buddy, and Dallas and Nico had done CPR on Jaydon in the water, fighting hard to save his life.

To no avail.

Dallas rubbed his aching shoulder again. The doc had told him he'd never have full range of motion, but he hadn't wanted to believe it.

Yet, seven months post-surgery and the reconstructed joint was nowhere near where he'd hoped it would be. He'd thought he'd be able to get back into life. Not as a Navy SEAL, as that was a young man's game, but in some sort of law enforcement.

He'd pretty much figured out retirement wasn't his thing. Responding to his sister's complaints wasn't enough either. He was growing bored, and that wasn't good.

Nico was searching for Jaydon Rampart's younger sister, Ava, who'd been missing for months now. Unfortunately, the trail had gone stone-cold. Nico had followed up a few leads that had turned up nothing useful. The last time he'd connected with Nico, his teammate had assured him he'd call if he found anything.

Still, driving between Austin and Fredericksburg was getting old. Maybe it was time to head back to San Diego. He keenly missed the ocean.

He instinctively slowed down when he saw several police vehicles off to the side of the highway. Something was going on. They were setting up a tent while buzzards circled overhead. The situation piqued his interest, but he kept going. Brenda was waiting. She wanted him to have another heart-to-heart talk with Jason.

When he came up behind another SUV, he decided to pass. There was no one coming the other way, so he moved over to go around it. But as he drove by, he did a double take when he glimpsed the driver.

Wait a minute, was that Maggie Stevenson? He lightly tapped the horn to get her attention. She turned and scowled at him, until recognition dawned in her eyes.

He smiled and waved, but she didn't return the gesture. Instead, she hit the gas, leaping ahead of him. A car was coming toward him, forcing him to return to his lane behind Maggie.

Her cold-shoulder reaction bothered him. They'd dated nonstop for three months between deployments. One night they'd gotten carried away, making it the best night of his life, followed by the one he regretted the most. He'd known that he loved her and planned to make things right, but he had urgently been called out to another deployment. That was how it happened sometimes with the SEAL teams. He'd promised Maggie he'd call when he was back stateside, but unfortunately, that hadn't happened for almost six months. When he'd finally gotten back on US soil, he'd called only to find out she was Maggie Chandler now because she'd recently gotten married.

Married. Despite what he'd thought they'd shared.

Fast-forward nine years to now. She was the one who'd found someone else while he'd been gone, so why had she looked so angry with him? Irritated, he followed her all the way into town.

To a small ranch house located on the other side of the city from where his sister lived.

He drove slowly past her house, wondering if he should get out and approach, when she got out of the car, slammed the door, and stalked down the driveway to the street. He hit the brake, stopping the car.

Maggie marched up to the vehicle, glaring at him as he

lowered the window. "What are you doing? Why are you following me?"

"Nice to see y'all, too, Mags."

Her brown eyes flashed with anger. "Don't call me that. Just tell me what you're doing here."

Romeo let out a whine as if he didn't understand why she was yelling at him. Frankly, Dallas couldn't quite figure out what had gotten her so riled up either. "Easy, Romeo, it's okay."

For the first time, Maggie seemed to notice the dog. Her features relaxed just a bit before her gaze turned back to him. "Well?"

"If you must know, I'm heading to my sister's place. When I saw you on the highway, I thought it would be nice to stop and say hey."

She narrowed her gaze. "After nine years of being who knows where, you just decided to follow me? To say hello? Do you think I'm stupid? I'm not buying your act."

"It's not an act." Dallas wasn't the type to get mad easily, but he felt his temper start to slip. "You don't want to talk, fine. I wasn't trying to follow or stalk you. I was just being neighborly."

"Neighborly?" Her face paled to the point he feared she might fall over. "You *live* here now?"

She looked appalled at the possibility. He couldn't figure out why she was acting so strangely. He was the one who'd been heartbroken. She was the one who'd moved on to someone else. He instinctively looked at her left hand; she wasn't wearing a wedding ring. Which didn't mean much.

"Dallas, are you living here in Fredericksburg?" she asked again.

"Not exactly, but lately I've been in town more often

than not. I've been helping my sister, Brenda. She's having some trouble with her son, Jason."

"Yes, I know Brenda and Jason, that's nice of you to help them out." She took a step back and forced a smile. To his eye, it looked more like a grimace. Suddenly she seemed nicer. "Well, it was great to catch up with you, Dallas. I'm sorry you caught me at a bad time, I—uh, need to get inside."

Before he could offer to meet her at a time that was more convenient, the front door of the small ranch house banged open, and a young girl came running outside. She wore a pink shirt, worn jean shorts, and flip-flops in deference to the heat. She had long, blond hair, pulled back in a ponytail, the same color and style as Maggie's. Which made sense when the girl shouted, "Mom! Nanna says to hurry up. Your spaghetti is getting cold!"

"Coming, Laney." The fake smile seemed frozen in place. "I really have to go. Bye, Dallas." She lightly ran toward her daughter, urging the girl toward the house.

"Who was that man, Mom?" he heard Laney ask. "Did you have to arrest him or something?"

"Oh, no, he's not a criminal. Just an old friend." Maggie opened the front door and nearly pushed the girl inside. Then she turned to look back at him for a long moment before she followed Laney inside, the door banging shut behind her.

Romeo let out a short bark as if asking what on earth was taking so long.

"Okay, boy. I hear you." He rolled up the window and put the car in gear. It seemed Maggie might have some role within the police department, considering her daughter's question about arresting him.

Had she come from the police scene he'd passed along

the way? It seemed likely. He hadn't seen a badge or gun, so maybe she had some other role. Or she was off duty.

Yet as he drove through town to get to his sister's house, he couldn't help but wonder if he'd really seen a flash of fear and apprehension in Maggie's dark brown eyes.

And if so, why?

CHAPTER TWO

Dallas Hoffman was in town. The revelation on the heels of stumbling across Tate's dead body was too much for her shocked brain to process. She hoped she hadn't given herself away, but there was no denying she had been caught completely off guard by seeing him.

"Mom? Is something wrong?"

She turned her attention to Laney. "No, sweetie. I'm fine. Tell me about your day."

"Me and Jane went swimming at Jane's house. It was a lot of fun," Laney said. "I wish we had a pool."

"We can't afford one, Laney," she murmured absently, taking a bite of her mother's spaghetti. Truthfully, she had been saving money for a new place, possibly one with a pool. But that wasn't pertinent. She hadn't told her mother or Laney the news about Tate. Maybe she was being cowardly, but she thought it would be better to give Laney the news in the morning rather than before bedtime.

It wasn't as if she'd have to leave early to get to work anyway.

Walking around without her badge and gun made her

feel naked. Especially not having the badge. She owned a backup piece, after all, this was Texas. Almost everyone carried or owned a gun, even in this small tourist town.

Including her mother. Not that Sarah had ever used the shotgun against another human being. But she had killed her fair share of snakes.

Maggie ate without tasting her mother's delicious home-made spaghetti sauce. Laney went on about their swimming afternoon, but she couldn't remember any of those details either. Laney ran outside to ride her bike while she helped her mother with the dishes.

"Maggie, what's wrong? You're completely distracted."

She froze in the act of putting a clean plate in the fridge, taking two steps to the side to reach for the cupboard instead. "Oh, I uh, yeah. Sorry."

"Trouble at work?" her mother asked.

She almost barked out a laugh, although the situation was anything but humorous. "Yeah, you could say that." She turned and went back to drying dishes. "Mom, I don't want to tell Laney until tomorrow morning, but Tate is dead. He's been murdered."

"What?" Her mother's eyes widened in shock. "How? When?"

"I don't know. I happened to find his body lying about sixty feet off Highway 16. I don't think he was out there for more than a few hours, but he was shot in the head, so it's being treated as a homicide. My boss took my badge and gun until I can be cleared as a suspect."

"Oh, Maggie. I'm so sorry." Her sweet mother quickly dried her hands and wrapped her arms around her shoulders. "That's so awful. First losing Tate, then being forced off work. Surely your boss knows you're innocent."

"I hope so." For a moment, she felt like a young girl

again, being comforted by her mother's embrace. She basked in her mother's support for a moment, then she stepped back and resumed drying dishes. "But guess who had an argument with Tate just last night over his desire to have Laney come to live with him throughout the school year?"

"That's not motive for murder," her mother protested.

Maggie knew from experience that people had been murdered for less. Then again, usually not in Fredericksburg, Texas. "Maybe not, but it doesn't look good. I'm hoping they'll soon find evidence that will clear me."

"What are you going to tell Laney?"

"I'm not sure." Laney would be upset, but possibly not heartbroken. Tate's fault for not spending more time with her. The child that was legally, but not biologically, his daughter. Texas state law didn't care who had sired the child, if the baby was born while you were married, you were legally deemed the child's parents.

But Tate, of course, knew the truth. And he'd proposed marriage, promising to love and cherish her and her unborn child.

A promise that had quickly eroded into bitterness followed by a series of affairs.

Her mind flashed back to Dallas. She hadn't seen him in the nine years since they'd spent the summer together.

Since the night they'd created Laney.

Up until now, she'd convinced herself she'd never see him again. That the issue of his being Laney's biological father didn't matter. She'd tried to get in touch with Dallas when she'd found out she was pregnant, only he was in some faraway country without access to phone or internet. Leaving her with two choices, either have Laney out of wedlock, bringing shame on her pastor father's reputation, or accept Tate's offer to marry him. She'd cared about Tate and had thought that would be enough to make things work.

She couldn't have been more wrong.

Still, she'd never anticipated seeing Dallas again. She knew his sister, Brenda, but they'd never been close friends. She wasn't sure if Brenda even knew about how close she and Dallas had once been. Brenda had been married and going through her own medical issues at the time.

Now Dallas was back. And knew where she lived.

Did he deserve to know the truth?

No, the better question was if Laney deserved to know her real father.

She didn't want to admit the answer was a resounding *yes*.

Ironic to realize Laney lost one father today but soon may have another father step in to take his place.

The thought of Dallas becoming involved in Laney's life filled her with dread. She didn't want to share custody. The way Tate had backed out of his responsibilities hadn't bothered her in the least. She preferred spending time, especially her weekends off work, with Laney.

"Don't stress, Maggie," her mother urged. "They'll clear your name and get you back to work in no time."

"I hope so." She quickly finished drying the dishes, then went outside to watch Laney. Her mother didn't know the truth about Dallas. Her parents had assumed she and Tate had gotten carried away and had married accordingly. Deep down, she was glad her pastor father hadn't known the truth before he'd abruptly died of a heart attack three years after Laney had been born.

"Look, Mom, no hands!" Laney lifted her hands off the handlebars as she cruised past on her bicycle.

"Be careful," she called, stifling a sigh. Times like these, she wondered if Laney got her daredevil persona from Dallas.

Out of the corner of her eye, she noticed a black car rolling slowly down the street toward Laney. Their house was located on the outskirts of town and normally didn't get a lot of traffic. Which was why it had been obvious that Dallas had followed her.

The house next door was empty, the owners renting it out as a vacation property. No one with any brains wanted to come to Texas in August, the hottest month of the year.

She instinctively tracked the car's movements. At first, she wondered if the driver was looking for the address of the rental property next door. Then she noticed the driver's side window go down, revealing the barrel of a gun. It was pointed toward her, not at Laney, but she could only think of her daughter.

"Laney! Stay back! Go back!" She pulled her weapon and hit the ground just as the sharp report of gunfire rang out.

She returned fire, mentally braced for the impact of a bullet. But the pain didn't come. Instead, the car picked up speed and took off.

A stunning realization hit hard. Someone had just tried to kill her.

"MAGS! LANEY!" Dallas had been walking toward Maggie's house when the near shooting event unfolded right in front of his eyes. He'd been too far away to do much more than fire his Sig Sauer at the black car to scare them off. And it worked as the driver hit the gas and the black car leaped forward. Dallas wanted to fire again, but his first concern was for Mags and Laney.

His initial anger over what he'd learned from Brenda about how Maggie had been pregnant before her marriage had instantly faded in the face of danger. He ran with Romeo at his side to where Mags was kneeling beside her daughter, who'd tumbled off the bicycle.

Our daughter, he mentally corrected himself. There was no doubt in his mind that Laney was his daughter. Something Mags had purposefully kept a secret from him.

"What are you doing here?" Mags snapped when she saw him.

"Who was that guy in the car?" he shot back. "Why was he pointing a gun at you?"

"Gun?" Laney echoed. "Who are you anyway?" The girl rubbed her scraped knee and turned toward Mags. "Mom, what's happening?"

Mags sent him a laser glare that could have fried him on the spot. He belatedly realized he should have chosen his words more carefully, but he wasn't used to being around kids. "There's nothing to worry about, Laney," she assured the girl. "This is Dallas Hoffman, remember, you saw him earlier? He's an old friend. How are you? It looks like you skinned your knee."

"Mom, was that one of the bad guys you arrested?" Laney persisted. Her dear tomboy daughter didn't seem to care that she was bleeding. "Is that why he came after you?"

"I don't know," she admitted.

Laney scowled, then looked again at Dallas, then down at the dog. The lab was sitting beside Dallas, his nose working the air. Dallas had trained with Romeo for months now, turning him into a great scent-tracking K9.

"I'm Dallas, and this is my partner, Romeo." Dallas

stroked the lab's head, then put his hand on Laney's arm. "Romeo, this is Laney." Then he did the same thing to Mags. "Romeo, this is Maggie. Friends, Romeo. Friends."

"He's pretty," Laney said, reaching over to pet him.

Dallas took the leash off so Romeo could play. The dog wiggled and wagged his tail with enthusiasm, trying to lick Laney's face. His daughter laughed, the sound beautiful to his ear.

Laney was adorable, smart, and spunky. His earlier anger swelled in his chest, threatening to choke him. He wanted to snap at Mags but battled the urge back. He didn't want to ruin this first meeting with his daughter.

His. Daughter.

Laney was enthralled with Romeo. She stood and idly rubbed her skinned knee, then ran into the yard, laughing when Romeo followed her.

"Who fired the shot?" Mags asked in a low voice. "You or the driver?"

"Me." He slid the Sig back into the holster. "I saw the gun and fired at the vehicle to draw their attention away from you."

Instead of thanking him, she scowled. "What were you thinking? You could have hit Laney."

"I'm a SEAL, I hit what I aim at," he drawled. "Our daughter was safe."

She froze, her mouth opening and closing like a trapped blue gill. He waited for her to tell him the truth, but she didn't. She stood and took several steps, putting distance between them. "Excuse me, I need to call this in."

"Hold on. Isn't it time to tell me the truth?" He didn't care if he sounded annoyed. He had a right to be upset. "I'm right, aren't I? You were pregnant when you got married. Laney is my daughter."

"Legally, she's Tate's daughter." Mags glanced over to where Laney and Romeo were playing. "You may be her biological father, but you forfeited that right when you left. I tried to call and talk to you, but I was told you were *unavailable*." She exaggerated the emphasis on the last word. "When I specifically asked how long you'd be unavailable, I was told *indefinitely*."

He couldn't help but wince. Imagining a pregnant Mags trying to find him only to be told those things was heartrending. If he'd known . . . no, there was nothing he could have done. Being a SEAL meant going on covert ops that no one could know anything about.

Not his sister, his parents when they'd been alive, or Mags.

Not anyone.

"Look, I'm sorry, but—"

"No buts," she interjected. "I was pregnant and alone, my father the pastor of our church. I did what I thought was best. Tate offered to marry me, and I accepted. It helped salvage my father's reputation, and that was important to me."

Reputation? More important than his knowing about his daughter? Dallas had to bite back a snarky response. He didn't care about her father's reputation, not when he'd lost eight years of his daughter's life.

Eight years!

He was about to say more, but Mags was making the call. "This is Detective Chandler. I'd like to report an attempted shooting incident that just took place outside my home."

He couldn't hear the other side of the conversation, but it was interesting to hear Mags identify herself as a detective. He'd known she was a cop and was suddenly ridiculously proud of the way she'd moved up the ranks to being a detective.

It also made him wonder about the scene he'd passed earlier that evening. She must have been there, but why hadn't she stayed to work the case? How many detectives did this small town have anyway? When he'd considered trying to enter law enforcement post-retirement, if his shoulder didn't keep him from passing the physical, he'd only considered Austin not Fredericksburg.

"Thanks." Mags slid the phone into her pocket. "A squad will be here shortly."

"Congrats on earning your gold shield."

"Thanks, I like my job." She avoided his gaze by looking over toward their daughter. It was a good thing Romeo liked to play because Laney and Romeo were chasing each other around the small front yard. "You can't just walk into her life, Dallas."

"Why not?" He tried to squelch the flash of anger. "I've already missed eight years, Mags. I'm not going to miss more."

She reached up to rub her brow, looking weary and frazzled. "There's a lot going on right now. I need you to give us a little time."

"Why? What could possibly be more important than me getting to know my own daughter?"

She finally turned to look at him. "I found Tate's dead body a few hours ago off Highway 16. He was shot in the forehead, and it's clear his death is being investigated as a homicide. I haven't told Laney yet that the only father figure she's ever known is gone forever."

"I saw the cops working the scene." He frowned. "Do you think this recent gunman is related to your husband's death?"

"Ex-husband. And yeah, the thought had occurred to me." Her expression was grim. "I don't have any idea what's going on, but hopefully once I've been cleared as a suspect, I'll learn more."

"How long have you been divorced?" God would not appreciate the way he was secretly happy to hear her marriage hadn't lasted and that her ex was out of the picture. Permanently.

"Four years. And no, I didn't kill him, and I have no idea who did."

"I never thought you had." He could tell she was upset about being considered a suspect at all. Yet it still burned that she hadn't waited for him. Hadn't believed in what they had enough to give it a chance.

All because her father was the church pastor.

"Thanks, but like I said, I need to have that conversation with Laney first. She's going to need time to grieve before I tell her about you."

It rankled, and he raked a frustrated hand over his short, blond hair. "Okay, I can see where that discussion should take priority, but don't make me wait too long. Now, let's talk about this recent attempt to shoot you. I don't think you and Laney should stay here alone. Whoever that was knows where you live. You and Laney need to pack a bag, and I'll take you to the closest hotel."

Mags shook her head, but the arrival of the squad prevented them from discussing his plan further. The officer who slid out from behind the wheel looked barely old enough to shave. Dallas came forward to stand beside Maggie as she greeted the officer by name.

"Hi, Waylon, thanks for coming."

"What happened?" Waylon's gaze bounced between the two of them. "You mentioned a shooter?"

Dallas inwardly sighed as the kid eyed his Sig. He was about to explain what happened, but Mags put a hand on his arm to stop him.

"Laney was outside riding her bike. I saw a black Ford sedan coming toward us, very slowly. Too slowly. The driver's side window rolled down, and I saw the barrel of a gun. I can't tell you the make or model, though. I shouted at Laney to stay away, then hit the dirt and pulled my weapon. I fired, but my aim was off. I heard gunfire, which turned out to be my friend Dallas Hoffman, and it was enough to scare the driver off. The last three numbers on the license plate were six five one."

The kid nodded, scribbling notes in his small spiral notebook. Dallas had to wonder if the kid was fresh out of the academy. "Two-door or four-door sedan?"

"Four-door." Dallas pulled out his wallet and showed the kid his ID. "I'm a retired Navy SEAL and carry a Sig Sauer along with a MK 3 knife. I saw the events unfold exactly as Mags—er—Detective Chandler described. I fired a round to scare him off." He frowned. "I should have aimed at the engine block. I have no excuse other than I was distracted by a personal issue and didn't really expect to see the gun in the first place." A lame excuse and proof that being out of the teams for eight months had already messed up his instincts. Once, he'd have dropped the driver without blinking an eye.

Ruminating over learning he had a daughter wasn't a good reason for a delayed reaction when seeing a gun.

"Wow, a SEAL, huh?" The kid eyed him with respect. "That's really cool."

"Thanks." He felt like the biggest idiot on the planet. He hadn't even gotten the license plate number the way Mags had.

Waylon took more notes. "Okay, I'll put out a BOLO for the black Ford sedan with the partial plate," he told Maggie.

"Run a DMV search on all the vehicles registered with that partial plate. Search within a one-hundred-mile radius, especially the Austin area, see if you can get a hit on the car. It may be a long shot, but it's a place to start."

"Right. Good idea." The kid nodded. "Anything else?"

"I need you to let Lieutenant Fernando know about this incident; it's possibly related to homicide he and Simmons are working."

The young officer's eyes widened. "Right. The homicide. Good idea. I'll call them right away."

"Great." Maggie stepped back, indicating the interview was over. Dallas was secretly surprised the kid hadn't questioned him more but decided that being a former SEAL had been enough to vouch for his character.

It wasn't the right attitude, anyone could turn bad, even someone who'd served their country in the military. It wasn't as if SEALs or any other special ops guys were immune to things like greed, jealousy, and power.

The kid hurried back to his squad and drove away. "Man, he's young," Dallas murmured.

For the first time since seeing Maggie on the highway, she cracked a genuine smile. "Barely twenty-two. He just finished his first year on the job."

Being thirty-nine, Dallas felt at least two decades older, if not more. Especially when his shoulder acted up. "I was a SEAL by then, hunting terrorists in the desert. Seems like a lifetime ago."

"I know." Maggie's smile faded. "Thanks for stopping by, but I need to get Laney inside."

He glanced over to where Laney was still playing with

Romeo. "I'm worried the shooter will come back. Will you please reconsider going to a hotel?"

"My mother lives here, and we're both armed. I'm sure we'll be fine."

"What about your dad?"

"He passed away five years ago." Her gaze reflected her sorrow.

"I'm sorry for your loss. But you need to let me sleep on your sofa." He reached out to grasp her arm. "Please, Mags. You can just say I'm an old friend and need a place to stay for the night. Which is mostly true as I was planning to drive back to Austin. I don't have an apartment in Fredericksburg."

She hesitated, then glanced back to where the car had been. "You can stay on one condition."

He knew where this was going and waited for her to say it.

"You will not tell Laney the truth. Not until I say it's okay."

He didn't like it but nodded anyway. "I won't say a word. I understand she needs to learn about her father's death." He hesitated, then added, "But don't drag this out too long, Mags. I don't deserve that and neither does she."

She looked like she wanted to argue, then she sighed and nodded. She turned toward the little girl. "Laney, time to put your bike away. We need to go inside."

"Aw, Mom. What about Romeo? Can he stay for a little while longer? Pleeaasse." Laney drew the last word out three syllables. He wanted to assure the girl she could play with Romeo as long as she wanted, but he knew better than to interfere with Maggie's parenting.

"Mr. Hoffman is going to sleep on the sofa, which means Romeo will be staying for a while too. But don't get used to this, young lady. Romeo is Mr. Hoffman's dog, not yours."

"Please call me Dallas," he said, smiling at Laney. "It's nice to meet you."

"Your dog is awesome," Laney gushed. "I love dogs, but Nanna says she has too much work to do without adding a puppy to the mix."

He wanted to assure Laney that she could take care of a dog without causing more work for her grandmother, but again, he held back. It wasn't easy, he wanted nothing more than to know everything about Laney. What she liked and didn't like. What activities she was involved in and her favorite subjects at school.

Dallas told himself to be patient. Two hours ago, he didn't even know about Laney. He'd asked Brenda about Maggie, and his sister had given him the scoop about Maggie being pregnant before the wedding, by at least four months. The timing was such that he'd felt certain the girl was his, and he had come here to confront Maggie.

It burned to know he'd missed out on so much. Thankfully, there was still time for him to get to know his daughter. No matter what Maggie thought, he was not giving up.

He put Romeo back on leash and followed Maggie and Laney inside the house. Mrs. Stevenson was in the kitchen reading a book. There was a flash of recognition in her eyes when she saw him.

He and Maggie had kept their relationship somewhat secret. Mostly because his schedule was unpredictable, and he could only get back to visit his sister for brief periods of time. He'd only met her parents once. But it seemed that was enough for Sarah Stevenson to remember him.

"Mom, this Dallas Hoffman and his dog, Romeo. He's an old friend and needs a place to crash tonight. You may remember him, and you know his sister, Brenda, she works at the gift shop in town."

"Sure, I know Brenda. Nice to meet you again, Dallas." A polite coolness underlined her tone.

"Laney, get our guest a pillow and a blanket, okay?"

"Okay, Mom." Laney bounced out of the room.

"Thanks for letting me stay." He glanced at Romeo. His K9 had his nose in the air, taking in the interesting and new scents.

The next thirty minutes contained awkward small talk. Finally, Sarah retired to her room, and Mags sent Laney to get ready for bed.

"Help yourself to whatever you need for Romeo," Maggie told him.

"Just water, I fed him at my sister's. I'll take him out one last time."

"That's fine, lock up when you're finished." She went around the house, closing the blinds. "Remember, I'm armed with my backup piece, and my mom has a shotgun."

"Good to know." He didn't doubt both Mags and Sarah could hit what they aimed at. But he wasn't going to let anyone get close enough that they'd need to. "Good night."

"Good night."

When he and Romeo were alone, he led the dog to the door. "Let's go, time to get busy." That was the key phrase he'd taught Romeo to encourage the K9 to go to the bathroom.

Romeo did his thing, and Dallas used his never-ending supply of eco-friendly baggies to take care of it. Dusk was falling now, the searing sun falling behind the horizon. He walked Romeo around the property, checking the layout of the house. This part of Texas consisted of wide stretches of flat terrain, some rolling hills in the distance. He'd left his car farther down the street, hoping he'd have a chance to talk to Laney privately, but the gunman ruined that plan. Now he headed over to drive it up to the house.

He was about twenty yards from his SUV when he saw a dark car coming down the street. It was hard to tell if it was the same make and model as earlier, but he broke into a run, determined to catch the guy to find out for sure.

Instantly the car stopped, then shot backward in reverse. He picked up his pace with Romeo at his side, but the car careened around a corner, shifted into drive, and sped away.

He caught his breath, staring at the car disappearing in the darkness. There was no doubt in his mind the driver had returned to finish what he'd started.

CHAPTER THREE

There was no way on earth she'd be able to sleep knowing Dallas was stretched out on the living room sofa. Maggie had successfully pushed him from her mind for nine years.

Or so she'd thought.

Now that he was back, memories cascaded over her. Great memories. They'd spent endless days together, talking, dining, riding, biking, swimming, and yes, had eventually slept together. It had been wrong to give in to their passion. Yet despite how alone she'd felt when she'd discovered she was pregnant and learned Dallas was unavailable on the other side of the world, she didn't regret having Laney.

Her daughter was the greatest gift she'd been given. The highlight of her life. She refused to feel guilty over bringing her sweet, smart, funny girl into the world.

Ironically, her regrets were centered around marrying Tate. It had seemed like a good idea at the time, a way to salvage her father's reputation and selfishly to protect her own too. Yet she'd immediately known she'd made a huge mistake.

She'd cared for Tate. As a fellow cop, he'd quickly realized what was going on when she kept having to pull the squad over to throw up. Her morning sickness had been awful, and he'd supported her through those times and more when he'd offered to marry her. She'd tried her best to make their marriage work.

But she hadn't loved him. Not the way a woman should love her husband.

Over time, that lack of love eroded their fragile relationship. Tate had grown moody, sullen, and eventually she'd caught him in bed with a bartender from a local pub, then with another woman too. When she'd confronted him, he'd tossed her pregnancy in her face. A truth she couldn't deny.

That had been the beginning of the end.

Now Tate had been murdered, a man with a gun had come to find her, and Dallas knew about Laney. In her wildest dreams, she'd never imagined even one of those things happening, let alone all three.

The gunman seemed to be the least of her problems. She felt more threatened by Dallas's demand to be a part of Laney's life. Maybe because the gunman threat was temporary, she had faith her fellow detectives would find him and the person who'd killed Tate, whereas Dallas's presence in her life was permanent.

Permanent.

A strange dizziness washed over her. The thought of seeing Dallas on a regular basis filled her with excitement commingled with dread.

A knock on her door had her bolting upright in bed. "Mags?" Dallas whispered.

She slid out of bed, tugging her baggy T-shirt down to cover her threadbare shorts. She opened the door, scowling at him. "What?"

"Pack a bag and one for Laney too. We can't stay here, I just saw the same black sedan."

The gunman had returned. Sobered by the news, she asked, "Did you get the full license plate number?"

"No, because as soon as the driver saw me, he put the vehicle in reverse and shot out of there. There was no front license plate, only a rear one. But it was too dark to see it clearly." He waved an impatient hand. "Come on, we gotta go. Get your mom too."

She hesitated, hating to admit he was right. "Fine. Give me a few minutes." Without waiting for a response, she shut the door and quickly changed her clothes. After tossing her overnight kit and a change of clothes into a small rolling suitcase, she went to wake Laney.

Her daughter was already asleep. She hated waking her, but there wasn't another option. "Laney, sweetie, you have to get dressed." She grabbed a clean set of clothes from the dresser and stuffed that into the suitcase too.

"Huh?" Laney blinked. "Is it morning already?"

"No, but we can't stay here. We're going to a hotel, won't that be fun?" She injected enthusiasm into her tone.

"Will Romeo be there?"

The little girl was becoming fixated on the dog. How much worse would it be once she realized Romeo's owner was also her father? Laney would be ecstatic. She shied away from the thought. "Yes, he's coming too."

"Okay." She scrambled out of bed and pulled on her clothes.

Maggie tossed Laney's swimsuit into the suitcase, secretly hoping for a pool to keep her daughter occupied, then rolled it into the living room. Dallas paced the small space as Romeo stretched out on the floor looking up at him. The moment Dallas saw her, he came forward to take the bag. Romeo jumped up to greet her, tail wagging with excitement.

"Good boy," she murmured, petting the dog. Then she straightened. "I'll get my mom."

The ranch house was set up so that the master suite was on one end, the two bedrooms she and Laney used were on the other. She hurried into the master suite. "Mom?"

"What is it?" Her mother hadn't been asleep yet either.

"I don't want to scare you, but the gunman returned. Dallas is taking us to a hotel. Can you please pack a small suitcase?"

"A hotel?" Her mother frowned. "I don't think that's a good idea."

"We can't stay here, Mom," she repeated firmly. "There's no time to argue. We need to go before anything bad happens."

Her mother huffed, then slid out of bed. "Fine. I'll pack a bag, but I don't like this, Margaret."

She winced. It was never good when her mother used her full name. "I don't like it either. I'm sure it won't be for long. The police know about the gunman and have a partial plate for the car. One or two days at the most and we'll be back."

"I hope so."

She hoped so too. Maggie returned to the living room to find Laney sitting on the sofa, her arm looped around Romeo. Dallas was watching the pair indulgently, and a flash of annoyance hit hard. There wasn't a doubt in her mind that he'd use the dog to influence his relationship with Laney. The girl hadn't been overly excited to spend time with Tate on those rare occasions he'd taken her. And when she'd asked Laney what they'd done, the only answer was watch movies.

Giving her the impression that Tate had simply let the girl watch TV all day and into the evening. So much for father-daughter bonding time.

What if Dallas demanded co-custody? It was clear Laney would jump at the chance to spend time with Dallas and Romeo. And there was no way Dallas would just let her sit and watch movies. He'd become the fun dad, the one who'd do whatever Laney wanted. Leaving Maggie to be the disciplinarian.

Her chest tightened with panic, but she forced it away. No point in borrowing trouble. Maybe Dallas would learn that kids were more work than he'd bargained for. As soon as the thought flickered through her mind, she knew it wouldn't happen. He was a SEAL. He'd thrive on the challenge.

Enough. There would be time to deal with that later.

Right now, the gunman was their main concern. She met Dallas's gaze. "Did you notify the police about seeing the car?"

He nodded, glancing at Laney. "Yes. They plan to keep searching for it."

"What car?" Laney asked.

Maggie was at a loss as to how to explain this in a way that wouldn't frighten Laney too much. "The car that came down the street earlier tonight showed up again. It's probably nothing, but we think staying at a hotel is our best option."

"But there was a man with a gun inside, right?" Laney persisted.

Dallas crossed to the sofa and knelt beside her. "There was a gunman, but when he saw me and Romeo, he took off like a scared rabbit. Don't worry, Romeo and I will keep you safe."

Laney managed a smile. "I won't be scared, not if Romeo is with me."

Maggie shouldn't have been upset at how much Laney already trusted Dallas and Romeo. As if having a criminal investigative detective for a mother wasn't good enough.

"Romeo likes you too." Dallas stroked the dog's sleek fur. "He's a good boy."

"Does he like to swim?" Laney's eyes were wide and bright with hope. "I love swimming."

"Romeo loves the water," Dallas assured her. "You should see him run and jump into the water when I toss a tennis ball."

"Do you live on a lake?" Laney asked.

Maggie knew this nonstop questioning could go on forever. "Laney, do you need to use the bathroom before we go? Nanna is here, and we're ready to leave."

Laney shook her head, but when Maggie gave her The Look, she sighed and slid off the sofa. "Okay."

As soon as Laney was out of earshot, her mother turned toward Dallas. "Is this really necessary?"

"Yes, ma'am. I wouldn't do this if it wasn't. I want y'all to be safe from harm."

"Harrumph." Her mother scowled. "I don't like leaving my home."

"I'll bring you back as soon as possible." Dallas turned toward her. "I'd like to take my SUV if you don't mind. Romeo needs the crate area in the back, and there are other features built into the vehicle for his safety."

For the dog's sake, she nodded. "That's fine. Thankfully, Laney is old enough that she doesn't need a booster seat anymore."

"Oh, ah—good." The surprise in his gaze indicated that possibility hadn't occurred to him. He obviously wasn't used to being around kids. "I'll take the bags out. I'll store them on the floor of the back seat."

Two minutes later, they were settled in Dallas's SUV. Her mother and Laney were in the back, leaving her to ride shotgun next to Dallas. The whole scenario felt a little too cozy for her peace of mind.

They were not a family heading out for a vacation.

She wore her backup piece, and she could see Dallas's Sig Sauer on his belt too. The situation was serious, and she turned to look at him as he backed out of her driveway. "Where are we headed?"

"There's a hotel on the north side of town that offers suites and a pool," he said. "I'd rather head toward Austin, but that should work for tonight."

"Yay, a pool!" Laney exclaimed.

"That's fine." She couldn't begrudge Laney the chance to swim, but she turned in her seat to eye her daughter. "No swimming tonight, though. There will be plenty of time to check out the pool in the morning."

"Aw, Mom," Laney whined. "Why can't I swim tonight? I'm not sleepy."

"Tomorrow," she repeated firmly.

Laney huffed but fell silent. Dallas looked at her as if he wanted to say something. When she narrowed her gaze in warning, he kept his mouth shut.

One night nine years ago did not give him the right to overturn her decisions. A fact he'd do well to remember.

The trip to the hotel was quick, and soon Dallas had arranged for them to stay in a large two-bedroom suite. He'd also insisted on sleeping on the sofa in the general living area with Romeo.

Her mother took one room, leaving the room with the twin beds for Maggie and Laney to share. Despite her claims of not feeling tired, Laney yawned and reluctantly agreed to lie down. Minutes later, she was asleep.

Maggie tiptoed into the living room where Dallas was opening the sofa sleeper. She winced, knowing it would be terribly uncomfortable for a man of his size.

He looked surprised to see her. "Do you need something?"

"We need to talk about the plan for tomorrow. I know checkout time is at eleven, and Laney will want to spend at least an hour or so in the pool. But what happens after that? We can't live in a hotel indefinitely."

"Not indefinitely, but we will stay away from your house until it's safe. It might be best for you to call the police department tomorrow to get information."

Since she'd already planned to do that, she nodded. "I don't know how much they'll tell me about Tate's murder. The two incidents must be connected, but I have no idea how."

Dallas put the sofa back together and gestured for her to sit. "When was the last time you saw him?"

"I haven't seen him in two years, but we did talk on the phone the evening before his murder." She frowned. "Maybe the person who killed him knew we had a conversation and is afraid Tate told me something he shouldn't have."

"Was Tate involved in something illegal?" Dallas asked.

"Not that I'm aware of, and if he was, he wouldn't tell me. I'm a cop. I'd arrest him myself in a heartbeat." As soon as the words left her mouth, she wished them back. Dallas's green eyes bored into hers as if he knew she hadn't loved Tate. She abruptly stood. "I need some sleep. We'll figure out our next steps in the morning. Good night."

"You can't run away forever," Dallas said as she headed

toward the bedroom door.

She glanced back at him, then opened the door and slipped through without responding.

No, she couldn't avoid him forever. This was nothing more than a brief reprieve.

Dallas's return had irrevocably changed her life.

THE SLEEPER MATTRESS was so lumpy Dallas had given up after five minutes. He stored it away in favor of stretching out on the too-short sofa. Granted, he'd spent worse nights on deployments, but his shoulder was aching worse than usual.

Romeo rested on the floor beside him. Dallas wryly realized Laney may have usurped him as Romeo's favorite person.

The brief conversation he had with Mags looped over and over in his mind.

I'd arrest him myself in a heartbeat.

He was secretly glad Mags hadn't loved her ex. But the news also made him frustrated. If only she had waited for him . . .

But then she would have endured her entire pregnancy by herself, given birth alone, and been a single mother with a newborn baby for who knew how long. As annoyed as he'd been to learn she'd gotten married, he couldn't begrudge her the partnership he'd been unable to provide. She had tried to get in touch, only to be told he was indefinitely unavailable.

Could he really blame her for getting married while carrying his child? His heart shouted yes while his brain told him no.

And really, it was his own fault for allowing himself to get carried away that night. He'd failed to maintain his tight rein of control.

Being a SEAL was all about protecting his country, yet he'd failed to protect Maggie. God would forgive his sin, but it wouldn't be as easy to forgive himself for his lapse in judgment.

Yet watching Laney with Romeo made it difficult to hang on to his disappointment and regret. She was so engaging and spunky, and he longed to spend every moment of every day getting to know her.

And as much as he admired Mags, he wasn't going to allow her to stand in his way.

Nothing on earth could make him walk away from his daughter.

He didn't sleep well, mostly because he kept listening for the gunman's return. They should be safe in the hotel, but their suite was on the ground floor with easy access to the indoor/outdoor pool. Maybe he should have insisted on connecting rooms located on a higher floor instead, but he'd wanted to make Laney happy.

He'd only just found out about his daughter, yet she was already impacting every decision he made.

By six in the morning, he gave up. Romeo seemed eager to go outside, so he put the lab on leash and slipped out of the room. He purposefully walked down the hall past the swimming pool, which didn't open until six thirty for guests. Laney would have to wait until after they ate breakfast to swim.

The exit door at the end of the hall led out back. The outdoor pool was to his left, so he went to the right to find a place for Romeo to get busy.

Maggie's question about next steps was a good one. He

didn't like being in the dark about what was going on. One thing the navy had done well was provide intel to their team while in the field. Yeah, sometimes the intel wasn't good or they lost satellite access, but knowing something was better than nothing.

He wanted to understand what Tate Chandler had gotten himself involved in. Criminal activity of some kind for sure. Innocent men were rarely murdered in small-town central Texas.

When Romeo was finished, he cleaned up the dog's mess and led him back inside. He frowned when he noticed the back door they'd come through had been left unlocked. He'd expected to need his room key to get inside. Not the best security in the world.

Maybe it would be better to take Mags, Laney, and Sarah to the house he was renting in a northwest suburb of Austin. It had a pool and was in a quiet neighborhood. He felt sure they'd be safe there.

Something to discuss with Mags before her mom and Laney woke up.

When he returned to the room, Maggie was sitting in the small living space. "I figured you'd taken Romeo outside."

"The joys of owning a dog," he admitted. "I'm glad you're up, though. I think we should head out to my place after touching base with the police. You, Laney, and your mom will be safe there."

"Your place?" She frowned. "You said you didn't live in Fredericksburg."

"I'm renting a house in a suburb of Austin. It's only twenty minutes from the Austin Medical Center and makes the trip here to Fredericksburg just over an hour."

"Tate was living in Austin. Or so he claimed. I was

there once when I dropped off Laney, but that was two years ago. He might still live there, or he might not. After finding him dead a few miles outside of Fredericksburg, I'm not sure what to believe."

"What was he doing for work?"

"He's a former cop but quit when we split. He told me he was providing security for some rich guy." She grimaced. "Unfortunately, I didn't push for more information. Our divorce was a bit difficult. We sold the house and split the proceeds, and since we were both working, I didn't ask for any alimony. He was supposed to pay child support, but that only lasted a couple of months. He so rarely took Laney that I didn't care."

"Child support." He felt as if he'd been kicked in the gut. "I'm the one who should be paying child support, not him."

"That's not how the court views things." She waved a hand. "It doesn't matter. We're talking about Tate and his living in Austin, not you."

They were, but it still rankled. "Could you find his house again?"

"Probably." She pulled out her phone. "I have his old address, so we can stick that in the GPS."

"All the more reason we should head toward Austin." Funny how he'd considered becoming a cop and here he was in the middle of a murder investigation.

Mags hesitated, then nodded. "Fine. But we'll have to come up with another plan once I'm cleared to return to work. Even if they don't let me work Tate's murder, I'll need to cover any other issues that arise."

He didn't know how many issues could possibly come up in a town the size of Fredericksburg, but he didn't voice his thought. "What about breakfast? I'd like to place an order with room service, but I'm not sure what Laney likes to eat."

"Room service is expensive," she protested.

"It doesn't matter." He owed her this and much more. "Please, Mags. I want to do this."

"Fine. Laney loves French toast as does my mom. I prefer eggs over easy with toast."

"I remember." Awareness shimmered between them for a long moment.

"Great. I'll get Laney up." She disappeared into the bedroom.

As he made the call, he added coffee with cream and sugar to the order, the way she liked it. He remembered everything about his time with Mags. The good and the bad. Mostly all good, though.

"Good morning," Sarah Stevenson greeted him cordially as she came into the room. Romeo instantly went over to greet her, tail wagging. He used to worry about Romeo being too friendly, but there was a time when some guy had tried to get in his face at the dog park of all places, and Romeo had growled, barked, and nearly bit the guy.

"Good morning. I ordered breakfast, it should be here soon." He couldn't deny feeling uncomfortable around Maggie's mom, too much guilt over knowing he'd gotten her daughter pregnant. "Maggie told me you and Laney like French toast."

"We do." Sarah petted Romeo, then moved farther toward him. "I hope you aren't planning to convince my daughter to move away."

What? Where had that come from? "I—uh . . ." He was saved by Laney running out of the bedroom.

"Romeo!" His K9 partner greeted his daughter with unabashed exuberance. "I've missed you."

"It's been less than eight hours," Mags said dryly. "I think you'll both survive."

Dallas hid a smile. When their food arrived, he fed Romeo, then joined the others at the table. Kaleb taught him and the rest of their teammates to pray before meals, insisting they should be thankful for their tasteless MREs, so he cleared his throat to get everyone's attention. "I'd like to say grace."

There was a long silence as Laney, Mags, and her mom glanced at each other. He could tell Sarah thought he was doing this for her benefit, but the reason didn't matter.

"Of course," Sarah finally said. She clasped her hands and bowed her head. Mags and Laney did the same.

"Dear Lord, we ask You to bless this food, bless this time we have together, and that You continue to keep us safe in Your care. Amen."

"Amen," they echoed.

"Can we swim after breakfast?" Laney asked.

"Sure," he said, then realized he should have let Mags answer. "If your mother says so."

"Yes, we can go to the pool for a while," she agreed.

He noticed Laney sneaking a piece of French toast to Romeo, who wagged his tail but didn't take the morsel. "No, Laney. He doesn't get people food."

"Why not?" she asked. "It's yummy."

"For one thing, it's not healthy for him. But mostly it's because I'm training him to only eat food I give him."

She looked crestfallen, and it was difficult for him not to give in. He realized Mags was doing a great job of being a single parent. Enforcing rules with his adorable daughter would take some getting used to.

"Okay," Laney mumbled.

When they were finished eating, Laney ran off to

change into her swimsuit. He pushed the small room service table into the hall, then escorted Laney, Mags, and her mother down the hall toward the pool. The hour was close to eight o'clock, and he figured they'd have a good hour or two of fun time before they'd have to head out.

Laney reached the pool first, with Mags following more slowly. Sarah hovered in the doorway, looking as if she wanted to talk, but he held up his hand, his gaze focused on Romeo.

The chocolate lab had his nose in the air, sniffing with interest. Out of nowhere, he began to growl.

"What is it, boy?" Dallas reached for his Sig just as the back door at the end of the hall opened, revealing a man with a gun.

Romeo let out a series of loud, sharp barks and ran toward the gunman. "No, Romeo!"

The gunman reared back from the dog, his body slamming into the door, but then slowly he turned the muzzle toward Romeo, an ugly expression on his face. There was no doubt in Dallas's mind that the gunman would kill the animal.

"Stop! Heel!" He fired a round, hitting the guy in the center of his chest. The momentum from the bullet sent the guy flying backward through the doorway. Romeo whirled on a dime and came running back toward him.

The dog was safe, but the gunman wasn't. Even from here, he could see the man wasn't breathing, thanks to the bullet lodged in the center of his chest. As Mags rushed forward, he wondered how in the world the gunman had found them at the hotel?

They should have been safe here.

Humbling to realize Mags and Laney wouldn't be safe until they figured out who was coming after them and why.

CHAPTER FOUR

The sharp report of gunfire had Mags grabbing Laney and curling her body around the young girl, shielding her daughter from harm. She turned to look at Dallas, shocked to realize he'd shot a man at the end of the hallway outside the pool area.

How had they been found?

"Mags! We need to get out of here."

What? She stared at the unmoving gunman. "We can't leave, you shot him. We need to call this in."

"We'll call on the way." There was a hard edge in Dallas's tone. "We're not staying here. Others could be nearby."

She forced herself to think about Laney. The little girl wasn't crying, but her eyes were wide, her face pale. "Okay, let's go."

Her mother nodded and moved close. Laney was so shaken by the gunfire she didn't protest about not being allowed to swim. The reality of the situation hit hard, and the little girl began to sob. Dallas held the door to the pool open, and Romeo wound around their legs as if reassuring himself they were unharmed.

The dog helped calm Laney. Dallas ushered them to their suite, then said, "Grab your stuff as quickly as possible."

It went against Maggie's nature to leave the scene of a crime. Not that she considered Dallas shooting a gunman in self-defense as a criminal act, but they needed to give the police their side of the story rather than run away.

"Come, Laney, I'll help you," her mother said, drawing Laney into the bedroom.

When they were out of earshot, she grabbed Dallas's arm. "We need to let the police know what happened."

"Not until you and Laney are safe." His grim expression convinced her that arguing was useless. "I shot him because he aimed his gun at Romeo."

She hadn't noticed that part. "Okay, fine. But this is only going to make us look guilty."

"Me, not you," he corrected. "Now get your stuff."

Her things only took a minute to gather because she hadn't unpacked anything other than a few toiletries. She tossed them back into her suitcase, then returned with Laney's bag to the main living area. Laney's eyes were red from crying, and Dallas was kneeling in front of her, talking to her in a calm, reassuring voice.

"Please don't be afraid, we're going to be fine, okay?" He lifted a hand to wipe at her tears. "Everything is going to be fine. Romeo is fine, and he's going to protect us."

Laney sniffed and nodded, resting her hand on the dog's head.

Maggie met Dallas's gaze. "We're ready."

He stood and turned toward them. "You'll need to follow me, we're not going out the main lobby door."

She'd expected as much. Glancing at her mother, the older woman nodded, indicating she understood as well. Taking her bag and Laney's, she fell in behind Dallas with Laney between her and her mom. Maggie knew her mother would protect Laney, and anyone coming after them would have to get through Dallas, then through her. There wasn't a doubt in her mind that Dallas would sacrifice his life for their daughter's if needed.

The way she would.

In that moment, she wondered if Tate would have done the same. Because despite his offer to marry her, he hadn't really bonded with Laney. It was why he'd barely made time for her.

Instead, he'd let the truth gnaw at him. Creating a bitterness that had eventually eroded their marriage.

She followed Dallas through narrow hallways until they found another side exit. Dallas held up a hand in a fist, indicating they should wait before he pushed open the door to peer out. When the coast was clear, he waved them forward. It was clear he'd done this often with his SEAL teammates.

His SUV was parked at the end of the lot. He hurried toward it, sweeping his gaze around as if searching for anything unusual. Squads flew down the road toward the hotel, but she did her best to ignore them. Dallas opened the back of the SUV for Romeo. She tossed their suitcases inside, then helped her mother and Laney get in. The moment they were settled, Dallas started the SUV, waiting for the police cars to converge in front of the hotel lobby before heading nonchalantly out onto the road.

Maggie was a little shocked at how easily they were able to slip away from the crime scene. The officers responding to the hotel should have noticed them and flagged them down. This was what happened when you had a police force that wasn't accustomed to major crimes.

"Where are we going?" Laney asked.

She exchanged a look with Dallas before turning to look at her daughter. "Dallas is taking us to his house in Austin, won't that be fun?"

"Is it safe there?" Laney asked with a frown.

"Yes, it will be safe there," Dallas answered.

"That's what you said about the hotel," Laney pointed out. "Why did the bad man come there anyway?"

"I don't know that yet, but we'll talk to the police about it very soon." Maggie tried to smile reassuringly, but Laney wasn't buying it. "I have confidence in the police department. I'm sure they will get to the bottom of this."

"I'm not going to lie," Dallas spoke up. "We are clearly in danger, and we don't know why. But I promise I will do everything in my power to keep everyone safe. Laney, Mrs. Stevenson, no one will hurt either of you while I'm here."

"Thank you, Dallas," her mother finally said. "And please call me Sarah."

He nodded, then turned his attention back to the road. From the way he kept eyeing the rearview mirror, she knew he was watching for a possible tail.

Or the police.

There were so many questions she wanted to ask but couldn't without scaring Laney more than she already was. Had Dallas recognized the gunman as the same guy who'd tried to come after her earlier? He had mentioned shooting him because the idiot had aimed at his dog, and she remembered hearing Romeo barking and growling. Yet how on earth had the gunman found them at the hotel? She pulled out her phone, staring down at the screen.

Her mind went back over the timeline. She argued with Tate at eight o'clock Tuesday night. On Wednesday, she found his dead body at three forty-five in the afternoon. By seven thirty in the evening that same day, the gunman drove slowly past her house, intending to shoot her. Dallas scared him off, but then he returned an hour or so later. She knew there was no way the gunman had followed them to the hotel. Dallas had been highly aware of that possibility and had kept his eye out for any sign of a threat.

Yet somehow the gunman showed up at the hotel at eight in the morning. Coming in the rear door closest to the pool as if he knew that was where they would be.

An educated guess as to their choosing a hotel with a pool because of Laney? Or was it possible Tate's killer had traced her phone? The guy may have known she and Tate had a conversation, assuming Tate had told her something he shouldn't have. Had he then used her phone to track her to the house, intending to silence her? Then when that had failed, he'd tried again, tracking them to the hotel?

Cell phones could be tracked via cell towers, but usually not to such an exact location. Her phone and Tate's had once been on the same plan, but not since their divorce. Was it technologically possible for the killer to have used Tate's phone to track hers? They had those find-my-phone apps built in, maybe Tate still had hers listed somewhere in his phone. She wasn't the most tech-savvy person on the planet, but the latter scenario seemed the most logical.

She opened her window and nonchalantly put her arm out, dropping the phone at the side of the road. No reason to take a chance if there was even the slightest possibility that someone was tracking her phone.

Better to cut all ties to her ex-husband.

Dallas glanced at her, lifting his brow questioningly. She shrugged and shook her head, indicating they'd talk more later. To his credit, he didn't push it. Maybe he'd already figured out the possibility of the killer tracking her phone.

The gunman was dead, but she didn't think that meant the danger was over. Quite the opposite. Then she had another thought. "Pull over."

"What's wrong?" Dallas asked.

"I want to check the SUV." She didn't say more because of Laney.

Dallas nodded and put on his hazard lights as he pulled off the road. They both got out of the car and did a quick sweep for any tracking devices.

Thankfully, they didn't find anything. Moments later, they were back on the road.

"What were you looking for?" Laney asked.

"I thought I heard something rattling. But everything is fine," she assured her daughter.

As she settled back against the seat, her thoughts returned to their precarious situation.

What had Tate gotten involved in? And if he was doing something illegal, or had stumbled across something illegal, why wouldn't he go to the authorities or warn her? Instead, he'd threatened to take Laney full time starting in September. Had said he'd sent her the paperwork to start the process.

Her stomach knotted with tension at the thought that her ex would put her daughter in danger. Maybe she hadn't loved him the way she should have, but she never would have done something so heinous as knowingly putting him in harm's way.

A flash of anger hit hard, and she turned to stare out the

passenger-side window to hide her reaction. It was one thing for Tate to resent her, to cheat on her, to avoid taking Laney for his assigned weekends, but this? Getting involved in something that brought a gunman to her doorstep, placing an innocent eight-year-old in danger?

Unacceptable.

He was not the man she'd thought he was.

They drove in silence for nearly forty minutes before Laney finally asked, "Dallas, does your house have a pool?"

Maggie suppressed a sigh. Dallas nodded. "Yes, there's a pool. I love to swim too."

"Really?" For the first time since the incident, Laney brightened. "Can we swim when we get there?"

"Ah, sure, if your mother thinks it's okay."

"Going for a swim sounds great," she readily agreed, wishing she'd thought to pack a swimsuit.

"How long until we get there?" Laney asked.

"Forty minutes now," Dallas replied. "Have you ever played the game I Spy?"

"Yes!" Laney eagerly sat forward in her seat. "I spy something red."

"The bumper sticker on the car in front of us," Dallas replied. "I spy something yellow."

"The car behind us," Laney said with glee.

Maggie found herself enjoying the easy way Dallas diverted Laney's attention from the seriousness of their situation. She'd fallen in love with him nine years ago but then convinced herself the feeling wasn't mutual and that it was time for her to move on.

But now she couldn't help but wonder what her life would have been like if she hadn't married Tate and had waited for Dallas. Would they have gotten married? Become a family? Would their marriage have survived the long deployments being a Navy SEAL required? Or would they have gotten divorced too?

There was no way to know. One thing was for sure, she couldn't have lived with herself if her father had lost his job because of her pregnancy. Her hasty marriage to Tate had caused enough of a ripple through their small community. Thankfully, she hadn't gained a lot of weight with Laney, so she was able to hide how far along she was.

Until Laney was born, then she could practically see everyone doing the math in their tiny minds.

Whatever. It was old news now. There was no sense ruminating on what might have been. She and Dallas couldn't go back and change the past.

Yet glancing at his profile, she was forced to admit she was thankful he was here now.

And she couldn't help but wonder if Dallas coming into her life when she needed him the most was exactly the way God had planned it.

DALLAS WAS SHOCKED when Maggie had subtly dropped her phone out the window. He hadn't really considered the possibility of being tracked by her device. She always seemed to be thinking ahead, that's for sure.

The other way would be for them to have somehow stumbled across his SUV. It was smart of Mags to think of a ⸻ker, although he didn't think there had been enough for that. But the gunman could have taken down the ⸻se plate number and searched all the local hotels to ⸻. A long shot, but possible. Going to Austin seemed ⸻e best idea. It was the Texas state capital, and without being followed, the bad guys would find it difficult to find them.

He kicked himself over and over for not being better prepared at the hotel for the gunman's reappearance. Something he absolutely should have anticipated. He made a silent vow to never make that mistake again. He needed to treat this entire situation like a SEAL op, which required coming up with several contingency plans.

When Laney grew tired of the I Spy game, he peppered her with questions about her favorite subject in school, what she liked to read, and anything else he could think of. He grinned like an idiot when she told him her favorite subject was science, her favorite color was yellow, and that she liked to read the Harry Potter books. Twice he caught Sarah's curious gaze on him and felt certain Maggie's mother had already figured out, if she hadn't known already, that he was Laney's biological father.

He desperately wanted to tell Laney the truth, but so much had happened that she still didn't know anything about her father's death. A situation he hoped Mags planned to rectify very soon.

"Hey, I remember Austin," Laney said, craning her neck to peer out the window. In the distance, they could see some of the skyscraper buildings. "I think I came to visit Dad here a long time ago."

Her innocent comment stabbed him in the chest like a knife. Tate Chandler might be dead, but he would always be Laney's father.

"That's right," Maggie said. "I dropped you off at his place."

"Yeah." Laney continued gazing out the window. "I haven't heard from Dad for a long time."

Beside him, Mags tensed, then casually asked, "Does that make you upset?"

Laney shrugged. "Not really. We didn't do much other than watch movies, and I'd rather hang out with my friends. Jane's swimming pool is great, and she always invites me over to swim."

"I'm glad," Mags murmured. "I'm sure he's been really busy."

"Probably," Laney agreed, seemingly unconcerned with the lack of seeing her father.

Maybe riding in the car wasn't the optimal place to have a serious discussion about death, but he shot Maggie an exasperated glance, wondering why she didn't say more. It seemed like the perfect opportunity. Especially when Laney was the one who brought up the subject of her father.

But Maggie remained silent on the subject.

Rather than going directly to his place, he drove in a wide circle around the surrounding streets, making doubly sure they weren't being followed. When he was satisfied nothing was amiss, he finally hit the button to raise the garage door and pulled inside. He closed the door before letting anyone out.

"Why don't you take Laney and your mom inside," he suggested to Maggie. "I need to let Romeo out. There are three bedrooms, you can have the master, your mom and Laney the guest rooms. I'll sleep on the sofa."

"It's your house," she protested, but he waved her off, opening the back hatch.

"Romeo and I won't be sleeping much anyway. Here, boy." The chocolate lab leaped down and looked up at him, tail wagging. "Let's go." He led the dog out the garage service door, leading to the rear side of the property. It was the same area where the screen-enclosed pool was located.

Romeo watered a few scrubby bushes, then came to walk beside him as he made a loop around the house. Again, nothing looked out of place.

He'd need to set up some trip wires and alarms to alert him if someone got too close. But he hesitated to take on that task in the daytime when the neighbors might see him. Better to wait until dusk had fallen.

Maybe he should get cameras, too, although he didn't want to leave Mags, Laney, and Sarah alone. Maggie was clearly the target here, and while she was a cop, he couldn't bring himself to leave her. The idea of losing her so soon after he'd found her again made him break out in a cold sweat.

He'd thought he'd gotten over her years ago. But seeing her now, he knew that was a lie. His feelings for Maggie had kept himself from getting too involved with other women.

Forcing himself to concentrate on the task at hand, he finished surveying the area, then returned to the house. Maggie and her family had made themselves at home.

Laney was still wearing her yellow swimsuit from earlier that morning. They hadn't taken the time to change their clothes. She was hopping up and down from one foot to the other impatiently. "Hurry, Mom, I want to swim!"

"Be patient, Laney." Maggie's voice was calm. "I told you we need to wait for Dallas."

"He's here!" Laney smiled when he and Romeo came inside. The chocolate lab made a beeline for the little girl. She dropped to her knees and enveloped him in a hug. "Good boy, yes, I love you."

"The feeling is mutual," he drawled, watching the pair

with a smile. "Come on, I'll show you how much Romeo likes to swim."

"Everything okay?" Mags asked, entering the open-concept living and kitchen area. The serious expression in her gaze told him she knew why he'd been outside.

"Yes, we're good." At least for now. He turned to head toward the screen-enclosed pool. Pushing open the sliding glass door, he gestured for them to head out.

Romeo darted past him and ran around the pool area until he found his orange rubber ball. Then he dropped the ball at Dallas's feet and sat, watching him expectantly. When he didn't pick up the ball right away, Romeo looked down at the ball, then back up at him as if to say, "What's your problem? Throw it already!"

He scooped up the ball and shouted, "Fetch," as he tossed it into the far side of the pool. Romeo didn't hesitate to jump into the water, swimming across the pool to get the ball. He could have run around the pool to get closer, but this was a training exercise they'd been working on. The K9 knew what to do. After grabbing the ball in his mouth, Romeo turned and dog-paddled back to the edge of the pool. Then he bounded up the concrete stairs leading out of the water, shook himself dry, and trotted over to drop the ball at his feet.

"Wow, he's so smart!" Laney exclaimed.

"He's well trained," Dallas corrected. "I've been working with him on this trick."

"Can I throw the ball?" Laney asked.

"Sure." He stepped back so that she could take his place.

"Fetch," Laney cried as she threw the ball. Romeo wheeled around and once again jumped into the pool. Dallas knew Romeo would fetch that ball for Laney until he was too pooped to swim any longer. Laney jumped up and down with excitement when Romeo dropped the ball at her feet.

"Hey, I thought you wanted to swim?" Maggie asked.

"I do. Fetch, Romeo." Laney threw the ball, then jumped into the pool behind Romeo. He'd expected her to doggie-paddle across the pool, but his daughter surprised him by performing an actual front stroke, cutting swiftly through the water.

"Did you teach her to swim like that?" He glanced at Maggie. "She's amazing for being so young."

"Not me, but I took her in for lessons. Had to drive into Austin, but it was worth it." Maggie shrugged. "She took to the water at an early age, and I wanted her to be safe when swimming with her friends."

Deep down, Dallas wanted to believe it was his genes that had contributed to Laney's swimming like a fish. He'd been the same way as a kid, always wanting to be in the water. It was one of the reasons he'd decided to join the navy out of high school.

Well, that and not wanting to work on the oil rigs like his father. He'd done that over his last two summers of high school and hated every moment. His friend had a ranch nearby, so he'd grown up taking care of horses too, but his dad had gone the oil rig route. The money was good, but no way was he going to spend the rest of his life doing that kind of work. His father hadn't understood, but in the end, he had been proud of him for becoming a SEAL.

"Maybe she gets that from you," Maggie said softly. "I can swim, but not like that. She knows all the different strokes already and likes to stay underwater for what seems like forever."

"I like to think she got that from me," he admitted. "I

was the same way at her age." He hesitated, then asked, "When are you going to tell her about Tate's death?"

Maggie was silent for a long moment, watching her daughter swim back and forth like a pro. "Maybe after lunch."

He tried not to sigh, but he was irritated at how she'd put the task off once again. He didn't understand why. It was clear from the conversation in the car that Laney hadn't seen her father in a long time.

"Would you like to swim?" he asked.

She blushed and shook her head, running a self-conscious hand over her cutoff jean shorts and simple T-shirt. "I didn't pack a swimsuit. Besides, I'm more concerned with what our next steps are in this investigation. It's hard to believe the gunman found us again. Now that Laney is preoccupied with Romeo and swimming, we need to call the Fredericksburg police to report the shooting."

He tried to ignore the stab of disappointment at not seeing Mags in a swimming suit. She was still stunningly beautiful, and there was no denying the attraction he'd once fought so hard to forget had returned with a vengeance. "Yeah, I know. Maybe you should call first, see if you can get an update on Tate's murder before we tell them about how I was forced to shoot the gunman. I only caught a brief glimpse, but it's likely he was the same one who drove past your house the night before."

"They already know about the gunman, we told them last night when Waylon responded to my house, remember?" She grimaced and added, "I'll call, but I need to borrow your phone."

"Not a problem." He unlocked his phone and handed it to her. They backed away from the pool area to make the call well out of earshot of Laney. Not that she was paying attention to them.

Maggie dialed a number, then held the device to her ear. "This is Detective Chandler, will you please patch me through to Lieutenant Fernando? Thanks."

He listened to her side of the conversation while keeping an eye on Laney and Romeo. The little girl held the ball over her head, and Romeo almost jumped on top of her to get it. Laney went underwater but then popped back up, giggling as she swiped the water from her eyes. She tossed the ball to the other end of the pool, then raced to swim after it.

She was a natural, and he loved watching her.

"Fernando, what's going on with the investigation?" Maggie asked. "Do you have a timeline of Tate's last-known actions the night of his murder?"

He couldn't hear the other side of the conversation, but Maggie frowned, indicating the news wasn't good.

"I'm sorry, I don't have my phone, but I already told you we discussed our joint custody arrangement. That call took place at eight o'clock in the evening. There's no way he was killed that early and dumped in the open range, the animals would have feasted on him all night."

Another long pause as she listened, then she said, "You know I didn't have anything to do with this, Loo. Why would I risk my job, my entire career, on him? I'd win full custody of Laney in a heartbeat if we took the case to court, and besides that, he hasn't paid any child support in over three years. He'd get dinged on that too. I'm sure he was bluffing about wanting custody, trying to get me riled up."

A spurt of anger hit hard on Mags's behalf. If Tate Chandler wasn't dead, Dallas would have found the guy to have a face-to-face conversation that would have put an end to this kind of nonsense. He didn't condone violence, but he also couldn't deny the urge to punch the guy for being such a jerk.

"Have you spoken to Waylon? The gunman showing up at my house must be related to Tate's murder. Like the guy knew about my last phone call with Tate and thinks I know something I shouldn't."

Another long silence as she listened to her boss. Her resigned expression was not encouraging.

"The gunman is the dead guy at the Longhorn Hotel outside of town. Get an ID on him and maybe you'll find your killer. Because it's not me, Loo. I had nothing to do with Tate's murder." This time, she didn't wait for a response, quickly disconnecting from the call. She handed him the phone, then lowered her face to her hands.

"Hey, don't lose hope." He didn't like seeing her like this.

"I don't understand why they're treating me like a suspect," she murmured in a low, agonized tone. "I've given eleven years of my life to serving and protecting the public. It makes no sense that one stupid phone call puts me at the top of their list."

He glanced over his shoulder at Laney and Romeo, who were still playing in the pool. Shielding Maggie from Laney's view with his body, he drew her into a hug. "You're not really a suspect, Mags. I'm sure they just don't want to risk influencing the investigation."

To his surprise, she leaned against him, accepting his embrace. "Logically, that makes sense, but I can't get over the way they're acting. As if we haven't known each other and worked together for eleven years."

She was taking the situation personally, and he understood her angst. He gently rubbed a hand over her back and pressed a kiss to the top of her head. After a long moment, she pulled away long enough to look up at him. It appeared as if she was going to say something, but then she suddenly went up on her toes and kissed him.

He was certain the kiss was meant to be a simple gesture of gratitude, but passion instantly sparked between them. And suddenly the kiss wasn't simple at all.

It was a sizzling reminder of everything they once had shared, along with the promise of so much more.

CHAPTER FIVE

Dallas's kiss sent the earth spinning like a tornado on its axis, bringing memories she'd long since buried bubbling to the surface. His strong yet tender arms cradled her close, his kiss curling her toes. She'd missed this.

She'd missed *him*.

"Mom, watch!" Laney shouted.

Hearing her daughter's voice was like being doused with a bucket of ice water. She broke free from Dallas's embrace and tried to catch her breath. The way she'd kissed him when her daughter was right there was horrifying.

The last thing she wanted to do was give Laney the impression that she and Dallas were a couple. Her daughter would be all over that like ants on honey.

"Coming!" She sidestepped around Dallas, avoiding his gaze. Laney was in the water holding the ball over her head. Romeo stood at the side of the pool watching the ball intently. When Laney tossed it up, Romeo jumped and caught it midair before landing in the pool with a splash. Then he swam toward Laney and dropped the ball in the water before her.

"Did you see that, Mom? Romeo is the smartest dog ever!" Laney exclaimed.

"He's amazing!" She smiled and clapped, inwardly relieved Laney had been preoccupied with the dog and hadn't noticed their kiss. But then she glanced over through the patio door and saw her mother watching with a frown.

Uh-oh. Busted.

She had never told her mother the truth about being pregnant with Dallas's child, too embarrassed to admit her mistake. Everyone assumed Laney was Tate's daughter. A logical conclusion as they'd gotten married.

Only now she couldn't help wondering if her mother had really believed Tate had fathered Laney or if she had known about her and Dallas. She had brought him home one night a month into their relationship, but then a few days later she had told her parents that Dallas was only in town short-term and would be heading back overseas.

Which is exactly what had happened, much quicker than either of them had anticipated.

After Dallas left, she buried herself in police work. Tate was a fellow officer, and they'd bonded over breaking up a bad fight and arresting the five people involved. He'd told her how impressed he'd been at her ability to hold her ground in the fight, and she'd been thankful for the recognition. Being a female cop in central Texas wasn't easy.

It was then she began to throw up on a regular basis, betraying her pregnancy, something Tate had quickly figured it out.

She did her best to thrust the memories aside, especially those featuring Dallas. She wasn't interested in becoming involved with him again. His insisting on being a part of Laney's life would be bad enough. Seeing him on a regular basis would be difficult, but she'd already gotten out of one bad marriage and wasn't about to repeat her mistake.

Dallas came to stand beside her. His unique musky scent was impossible to ignore, although she tried her best. His low, husky voice rumbled near her ear. "I love watching Laney. You did an incredible job raising her."

A lump lodged in the back of her throat. She managed a nod in agreement. Because Laney was a great kid. A handful at times, but still wonderful.

"Maggie, do you have a minute?"

Her mother's voice snagged her attention. "Of course." She left Dallas watching over Laney, knowing he wouldn't let anything happen to the girl, and joined her mother inside. She closed the patio door behind her. "What is it?"

"Is Dallas Laney's father?"

The blunt question shouldn't have surprised her, but she didn't have a snappy comeback. She looked at her mother for a long moment, then nodded. "Yes. Dallas figured out the truth too, but we aren't going to tell Laney until later. I need to talk to her about Tate's death first."

"I've always wondered," her mother murmured. "I never saw you look at Tate the way you looked at Dallas."

She flushed and sighed. "I tried to reach Dallas when I learned I was pregnant but was told he was indefinitely unavailable. When Tate offered to marry me, I figured it was the best thing for everyone involved."

"Only it wasn't," her mother said softly. "Your divorce after four years of marriage proved that."

"I know." Maggie decided not to mention how she'd also wanted to salvage her father's reputation, along with her own. "I need to talk to Laney about her father very soon. I hate to ruin her appetite, so I'm planning to do that right after lunch."

Her mother lifted a brow. "I'm not sure Laney will be too upset as she hasn't seen him in so long."

"You may be right, but the concept of death isn't easy to explain to an eight-year-old. That part may bother her the most."

"I agree, but we've always taken Laney to church, so she knows about God and Jesus. We talked to her about that after your father died. We'll just let her know her father has everlasting life with our Lord." Her mother made it sound so simple when it really wasn't.

Tate had attended church with them the first two years, but then he had stopped. She'd known then that he'd only gone in the first place to make her happy, not because he truly believed in God and the power of prayer.

It wasn't her choice to make, so she'd let it go. Tate may not have been a true believer, but to go from a cop to getting involved in something criminal was entirely different. Yet the gunmen coming after her proved he must have gone down a very dark path.

Doing what? She had no idea even where to begin.

"Maggie, don't put the conversation off too long," her mother advised. "Dallas is here now and seems to be interested in being a true father to her. She deserves to be loved and cared for the way Tate never did."

She nodded, understanding her mother was right. Time to stop being selfish and to concentrate on her daughter.

And Dallas.

After almost ninety minutes of swimming, Maggie told Laney it was time to get out. Her daughter didn't put up a fuss, maybe because Romeo had already given up playing and had stretched out on the concrete to rest.

After drying Romeo with a towel, Dallas tossed a frozen pizza into the oven for lunch. Maggie convinced Laney to change into shorts despite Laney's insistence that she wanted to swim again later. Fifteen minutes later, they sat down to eat.

This time, she wasn't surprised when Dallas bowed his head to say grace. "Dear Lord, we thank You for keeping us safe in Your care. Please continue to shelter us from those who seek to do harm. Amen."

"Amen," she echoed. Laney and her mother also repeated the sentiment.

"Does Romeo know other tricks?" Laney asked after inhaling her first slice of pizza. "You must have trained him to do more than chase a ball."

"I have done a lot of training with him," Dallas said with a smile. "Mostly obeying commands and finding specific scents. He's coming along very well."

Maggie glanced at him in surprise. "Are you training him to work as a police dog?"

"Most police dogs have to be trained by professionals, but yeah, that was the general idea." He shrugged and reached up to massage his left shoulder. "I had surgery earlier this year, and the recovery is taking way longer than I'd hoped. My goal of joining a police force isn't looking so good."

Her jaw dropped. "I had no idea you had surgery and wanted to be a cop!"

He instantly dropped his hand. "I'm fine. Just took a load of shrapnel in my shoulder on our last op. It's not a big deal."

Obviously, he was downplaying the injury, maybe for Laney's sake. Still, she couldn't help but wonder what else she didn't know about him.

Had he been married before? Engaged? He didn't wear a wedding ring, but neither had Tate. Her ex-husband had tattooed her name on his arm, though, something she'd secretly abhorred. Especially since Tate seemed put out that she wasn't interested in returning the favor. As if a tattoo was a sign of undying love. Yeah, not. Thank goodness she hadn't.

"Can I help you train Romeo?" Laney had a one-track mind, and it was centered on the chocolate lab. "Please?"

Dallas hesitated. "You can watch me train him, but he needs to learn to only listen to my commands, not anyone else's. I'm sorry, Laney. You can't be involved in that way."

The little girl looked disappointed. "I understand," she said glumly.

Maggie had to give Dallas credit for not giving in and granting their daughter's every wish. Laney had to learn she couldn't have everything she wanted.

When they finished eating, her mother rose to clear the table. Dallas stood, and Laney was about to leave, too, but she put a hand on her daughter's arm. "Laney, we need to talk. I have some bad news for you."

Instantly, her daughter looked frightened. "Is the gunman coming back?"

"No, sweetie. This is about your father." She hesitated, glancing over to where Dallas stood near her mother, then said, "I'm sorry, but your dad died."

Laney wrinkled her brow in confusion. "Is that why I haven't seen him in so long?"

Oh, it was tempting to say yes, but she couldn't lie. "No, Laney. That's not the reason. Your dad died yesterday. We don't know much about what happened. I wanted to tell you earlier, but things have been a little busy."

Laney was silent for a long moment. "Is he going up to heaven to be with Papa?"

"Yes, absolutely." She hugged Laney's thin shoulders.

"Don't be sad, Laney. Your dad is in a much better place now."

Laney clung to her for a long moment. "Mom, was it my fault Dad didn't come to see me?"

"Oh, honey, no! Absolutely not!" Maggie was horrified her daughter was taking responsibility for Tate's shortcomings. "Your dad just got too busy, it was nothing you did."

Laney didn't look convinced, and she looked over to where Dallas stood, his features a grim mask. She sensed he would have liked to punch Tate in the nose, but of course, that was impossible.

As if sensing the little girl's distress, Romeo came over to lay his head on her lap. The action made Laney smile. "Good boy, Romeo."

"Hey, do you want to watch me do a quick training session now?" Dallas asked.

Instantly, Laney brightened. "Yes!"

"Follow me." When Dallas lifted his hand and brought it to the center of his chest, Romeo trotted over to his side. He showed Laney a few commands, and soon Laney seemed to forget all about her father's lack of seeing her and his untimely death.

A man reaps what he sows. The Galatians Bible verse her father often used in his sermons popped into her mind. The sentiment was appropriate for this moment.

It was Tate's fault Laney wouldn't grieve for him.

A completely opposite situation from today. Laney had already bonded so closely with Dallas and Romeo, that if Dallas abruptly left, their daughter would be destroyed.

DALLAS WAS glad he was able to distract Laney from her sadness, which was less about her father dying and more about feeling guilty for something she assumed caused his lack of being an upstanding parent.

He'd managed to control his anger, using Romeo to help lighten the moment. Soon, Laney was distracted by a video game Maggie's mom had brought along, giving him some alone time with Mags.

"What do you think about getting cameras up around the exterior of the house?" he asked in a low voice. "I want to set up some trip wires too."

She nodded thoughtfully. "Those are both good ideas, and I'd also like to drive past Tate's house. I'm sure the cops have it staked out, but we can drive past without alerting any suspicions."

He frowned, considering their options. "I don't want to leave you, Laney, and your mom alone, so we either go together or not at all."

Maggie didn't answer right away. "I hate to admit it, but you should probably go alone. We know we weren't followed, which is good. It shouldn't take you too long to get what you need and to swing by Tate's place."

He lifted a brow in surprise. "Are you sure? I'm not convinced leaving you here alone with Sarah and Laney is the best idea."

"I'm an armed cop. I can protect my family." She narrowed her gaze as if waiting for him to claim he could protect them better than she could, then waved a hand. "You're better off buying the stuff you mentioned. I've never purchased cameras before."

"Okay." It was shockingly hard to leave, but the sooner he picked up the supplies he needed, the better. He stood, then asked, "Does your mom have a cell phone? I'd like to be able to stay in touch."

"She does." Maggie rattled off the number so he could enter it into his phone. "Laney doesn't have one, and don't even think about getting her one, Dallas. No eight-year-old needs a phone."

"I tend to agree. But I'll pick up one of those disposable phones for you to use in the meantime."

"That's a good idea." She glanced over to where Laney was playing a video game with the lab stretched out beside her. "Are you leaving Romeo here or taking him with you?"

"I'll leave him with you." The K9 would be one more added layer of protection. One he hoped wouldn't be needed. "I'll be back as soon as I can."

"I know."

He headed toward the door leading into the garage. He'd barely opened it when Maggie cried, "Oh, wait, let me give you Tate's address."

He turned, and the way she hurried over to his side made him yearn to sweep her into his arms for another kiss. How he managed to hold back, he had no clue. She took his phone and quickly typed it in. "There."

"Thanks." He stared down at her for a long second, desperately wishing he had the right to hold her close. After a moment, he crossed the threshold, closing the garage door behind him.

After backing out of the garage, he closed the door, then headed toward Tate's house. He figured the drive-by wouldn't take long, especially if the cops were still processing the place for evidence to the guy's murder.

To his surprise, the house appeared vacant, no sign of police or any other law enforcement. It made him wonder if Tate hadn't been living there at all. Mags indicated it had been two years since she'd been there. The guy could have easily moved someplace else in that time frame.

He drove past twice, then headed toward the closest big box store to get the phone and cameras. Every minute he was away from Laney and Mags was agonizing. He kept his phone close, half expecting Maggie to call on her mother's phone to let him know they'd been found by the gunman.

He made two more stops to get fishing line and to pick up more food before heading back. As earlier, he made sure there was no one following him, frequently changing direction and taking last-minute turns.

When he pulled up to his rental house, he was relieved it looked the same as when he'd left a little over an hour earlier. The garage door opened, and he drove inside, then quickly closed it. He grabbed the food first and headed inside.

"Mags? Laney?" he called. Laney jumped off the sofa as Maggie came out from one of the bedrooms.

"Can I go swimming again, Dallas? Mom said I had to wait for you to get back."

He was surprised she was so ready to jump back into the pool. No wonder parents always looked so exhausted. Laney contained boundless energy in her wiry frame. "Ah, maybe in a little while. I have a few things to take care of first."

Laney's shoulders slumped, and she grimaced. "Okay."

Man, he hated disappointing her. Yet he needed to get a few things accomplished, like putting the food away, activating Maggie's phone, and setting up the cameras and the video program that will be linked to his phone.

"Why don't you watch a movie?" Maggie suggested. "I'm sure we can find something of interest."

"I guess," Laney muttered. "I should have brought more books."

"I have a small tablet," he offered. "I will happily download some books for you to read."

"Really? Okay!" Laney brightened. "Let's see if there's a good movie on first."

He watched her head over to the television. Maggie joined her, manning the remote and clicking through the channels. He put the groceries away, then went back to the garage to get the rest of the stuff he'd purchased.

They must have found something they liked because they settled on the sofa. As he worked, he found himself smiling at how they seemed like a family. It made him long to tell Laney the truth, but he knew Maggie was right about waiting a bit.

Soon, though. He was going to insist they talk to her about his role in her life from this point forward very soon.

When he had the camera system operational, he decided to start putting them in place. There had been no sign of his neighbors, and he figured midafternoon as the hottest part of the day was the best time to get the task accomplished. Most people who lived in this area stayed indoors as much as possible during the hot August days.

He'd already pinpointed the locations in his mind, so it didn't take him long to get them mounted in obscure corners of the property. When that was finished, he added the trip wires. He avoided the areas Romeo used to get busy and made a note to make sure the K9 didn't get hurt by them.

Satisfied with what he'd accomplished, he nodded at Maggie to let her know Laney could swim anytime. He saw Sarah poking around in the kitchen and told her to help herself to whatever she wanted.

"I thought I'd throw together grilled sandwiches for

dinner." She met his gaze, but then quickly looked away. "I'm used to cooking for Laney and Maggie."

"Sounds great to me," he said. "Thanks."

She abruptly turned to face him. "I know the truth."

He froze, his mind whirling. Had Maggie told her or had she simply figured it out on her own? "I—uh . . ."

"You shouldn't have left her," Sarah said. "Not without some way for her to contact you."

"Being a Navy SEAL," he began, but she cut him off.

"You should have been more responsible," she insisted. "Your carelessness put Maggie in an impossible situation."

"You're right," he said quietly. "There is no excuse. All I can say is that I'm sorry."

Sarah stared at him for a long moment before saying, "Don't hurt her like that again."

"I won't." The words came easily but also gave him pause. The way she'd kissed him earlier had made him consider the idea of giving their relationship another try. They were both older and wiser, so they wouldn't make the same mistakes they had nine years earlier. And there wouldn't be any more deployments to keep them apart either.

Yet there was Laney to consider now. A little girl who didn't know he was her real father. And what if things between him and Maggie didn't work out for some reason? That would make their situation that much more compli-cated. Laney may even be upset with him on her mother's behalf.

No, he couldn't take the chance of losing Laney.

It hurt, but he told himself there could be no more kiss-ing. Or hugging. Or reminiscing about the past.

He couldn't allow anything to distract him from the

precious time he had left with his daughter. He'd already missed eight long years.

"I like the book better," Laney said as Maggie turned off the television. "The characters are fun, but they left so much out when they made the movie."

"Harry Potter?" he guessed.

"Yep." Laney grinned. "We only saw the second half of the movie, but that's okay because I saw it before."

"Many times," Maggie drawled.

Romeo stretched and came over to join them, tail wagging as if he knew there was more fun to be had. One thing was for certain, the K9 would sleep well tonight. Between his training and Laney's playing, Romeo was getting a good workout.

"Time to swim," he announced with a grin. Laney let out a whoop and ran to the bedroom to change.

"I see you have everything set," Maggie said.

"Yes. I'll show you how it works, oh, and here's your new phone." He handed her the small device. "You'll need to activate and charge it. Sorry, it's nothing fancy."

"That's fine. I wasn't expecting it to be a smartphone." She leaned forward to see the screen on his device. The first camera overlooked the driveway. He clicked on the screen to show her the street in front of the house was empty.

"The cameras are triggered by motion. But I can also scroll through to see what's going on outside too." He demonstrated for her. "I set up trip wires, so don't let Laney run around outside by herself. She'll have to stay in the house and in the pool area."

"She's loving it so far, but I know she'll get bored soon," Maggie warned. "She'll want to see her friends sooner or later."

"I know. We'll have to pray the Fredericksburg police

are able to ID the gunman and somehow trace him to Tate's murder."

"And if they don't?" Maggie asked.

"I may have to call in my SEAL buddies to help." He was hoping to use them as a last resort, mostly because Mason, Kaleb, Hudson, and Dawson were all old married men now, preoccupied with their new lives outside of the military. Nico was a possibility, but he was still searching for clues to Ava's disappearance, and Dallas didn't want to take him away from that task. Ava was Jaydon's sister. Jaydon and Nico had been swim buddies, and he knew Nico would never give up searching for Ava.

"What can they do? A better idea is for me to go back to work so I can investigate the case myself," Maggie said. "I'm the one who is at risk here. I'm going to call my boss again later to insist he reinstate me."

"He won't do that until you're cleared," Dallas reminded her, squelching a flash of fear. "Please, Mags, don't put yourself in the killer's crosshairs. Let's stay the course and see what happens, okay? One night of being safe isn't much to ask."

"Okay, fine. But we can't just hang out here playing house forever." She turned away as Laney ran back into the room. "Looks like you're ready to go."

"Can Romeo swim with me again?" Laney asked.

"Sure." He found it difficult to refuse the little girl anything. "But if he gets tired, let him rest."

"I will. Come, Romeo!" Laney rushed through the patio doors, then jumped into the pool, making a huge splash. The chocolate lab didn't hesitate to follow her in.

The rest of the evening passed without incident. Laney swam until close to dinnertime. Sarah kindly cooked, then shooed them into the living room to watch another show.

When Laney's eyelids began to droop, Maggie insisted it was time to get some sleep.

When the women were tucked away in their respective rooms, he pulled out his phone and flipped through the cameras. He didn't see anything unusual. Still, he'd sleep on the sofa, just to be on the safe side. Once darkness fell, he stood and moved toward the garage door. "Come, Romeo."

The chocolate lab was sprawled on the floor. The K9 opened one eye, looking at him as if to say you've got to be kidding. Apparently, Laney had worn the dog out big time.

"Romeo, come." This time, the lab responded to his stern tone. He uncurled himself, stretched, then came to sit at his side. "Good boy."

Moving silently through the garage, Dallas went out the back door to the yard. He told Romeo to get busy as he scanned the area. The dog quickly did his thing, and after taking care of the mess, they went back inside.

They hadn't been followed, and he had cameras and trip wires. They were safe.

He hadn't gotten much sleep the night before, so when he stretched out on the sofa, he closed his eyes and was out like a light.

His vibrating phone woke him up. He instantly grabbed it and saw that the front camera overlooking the street had been activated.

A black car slowly passed the house. The tinted windows made it impossible for him to get a good view of the driver.

He stared at the screen until the car was out of sight. Then the camera went dark. He waited for long, interminable moments to see if the vehicle returned.

Five minutes passed. He was just about to set the phone aside when it vibrated again. He swiped at the screen and saw what looked to be the same vehicle drive past from the other direction.

A coincidence? No way.

He felt certain the gunman was either looking for them in the general area or knew exactly where they were.

CHAPTER SIX

It was too early for her to go to bed, and hiding in her room to avoid Dallas was just plain stupid. Maggie silently made her way into the main living area, trying not to disturb Laney or her mom.

Dallas stood to the side of the window overlooking the front yard, staring into the darkness. Romeo was asleep on the sofa. She would have sworn she hadn't made a sound, especially since the chocolate lab didn't move, but Dallas turned to look at her. "I thought you were asleep," he whispered.

"I'm not." She edged closer. There had to be a reason he was staring outside. "What's wrong?"

"A dark car just drove by, twice in a seven-minute time frame." He held up his phone. "I managed to get a picture of it, but the angle makes it impossible to make out the license plate."

She thought about the dark car that approached her house and the partial plate she'd caught. "The previous car's last three digits were six five one."

"I remember." He scrolled through the phone. "Here, see what you think."

The video was still in the phone's memory. She started the feed and watched the car slowly roll past the rental house. The angle did make it difficult to see the plate. Even knowing the last three numbers of the other car, she couldn't say this was the same one. The second video was recorded seven minutes later when the car returned from the opposite direction.

Feeling grim, she handed the phone back to him. "It's possible the car doesn't belong to the gunman."

"I thought about that, the driver could have dropped someone off, then left the neighborhood, but I can't afford to ignore the possible threat." Dallas sighed and rubbed the back of his neck. "What I don't understand is how they could have possibly found us here?"

She nodded slowly. "I thought for sure they tracked my phone to find us at the hotel. Is it possible they know your vehicle?"

"I considered that. We weren't followed, and the SUV has been in the garage the entire time, except for the two hours I was out picking up supplies." His eyes flashed with frustration. "This doesn't make sense. No one should be able to link me to you."

"True." Dallas had popped back into her life after Tate had been murdered. Tate knew the truth, but why on earth would he have mentioned it to someone else after all this time? Especially since Tate hadn't known Dallas was back.

Except Dallas had been driving between Austin and Fredericksburg to help his sister.

"How long have you been back in Texas?" She gestured to his arm. "You mentioned surgery on your shoulder in January, have you been here since then?"

"Yeah, I had surgery at the VA center in Austin. It was the closest medical center to my sister, and as I said, I'm still getting some physical therapy."

"Is it possible you ran across Tate within the past few months?"

Dallas shrugged. "No clue. I don't remember meeting anyone by that name. I don't know what he looks like."

"Red hair, trimmed red beard."

Dallas shook his head. "Doesn't sound familiar."

She nodded, thinking back to those intense weeks she'd spent with Dallas nine years ago. It's possible they'd run into Tate at some point, Fredericksburg wasn't that big. Yet that was also during the height of the tourist season. "He may have seen us together back then."

"Maybe, but why does it matter? Tate's murder has nothing to do with me. Or you," he added.

"I know, but there must be something we're missing." She wished, more than ever, she could have been a part of her ex-husband's murder investigation. "I can't figure out how this house rented under your name was found by the gunmen."

"The only possibility I can come up with is that they took down my license plate number that first night outside your house." Dallas scowled. "Getting access to DMV records is no easy task. Only someone with connections could do that."

Nausea churned in her belly. "Tate was a former cop and obviously had already been murdered by then. However, there could be other cops involved. Maybe Austin police."

"You need to find out if the Fredericksburg police found anything while digging into the partial license plate."

She grimaced. "I can try, but I'm still being treated as a suspect."

"I get it, but we need to know if they found the vehicle or have gotten the ID on the gunman."

Dallas was right. She stared at her disposable phone, wondering if she could find a way to talk to Waylon personally. The guy worked second shift, so he was likely on duty now. She dialed the dispatcher and requested to be put through to Waylon Rutgers.

"What is this regarding?" the dispatcher asked.

Maggie hadn't identified herself as a detective, and the disposable phone number she was calling from added another layer of anonymity. "A personal matter."

"Hold, please."

After a brief wait, the young rookie picked up. "This is Officer Rutgers."

"Waylon, it's Maggie Chandler. I'm sorry to bother you, but I need to know if anything came of the partial license plate I gave you last night. A dark car has driven by my new, and secret, location. Now I'm worried the gunman has found me and my daughter." She shamelessly played the female card, hoping if he had been told to freeze her out of the information loop that he'd give her something anyway.

"I turned a list of twenty possible vehicles over to the lieutenant," Waylon informed her. "He was in the process of running them down."

Rats! "Oh, Waylon, would you be willing to share that list with me? I'm afraid my daughter is in danger."

She held her breath at his long pause. Then he sighed. "Yeah, I'll send it. You want it to go to your email?"

"No, but I'll give you a phone number to text it to." She looked at Dallas who whispered the number. She repeated it for the young officer. "Thanks, Waylon. You're a lifesaver. I can't bear the thought of anything happening to Laney."

"Stay safe, Maggie. They found a dead guy at a hotel this morning. That's two homicides in our small town in two days."

"Really?" She knew it was only a matter of time before Fernando learned that Dallas had killed the man. "Did they get an ID on him?"

"Yeah, David Cortney," he said. "Heard he's from Austin."

"David Cortney," she repeated for Dallas's benefit. "Doesn't sound familiar."

"From what I hear, no one has heard of him. Loo thinks the two killings are related as both of the deceased were from Austin."

"Wow, I wish I was there to help out." As soon as the words slipped from her mouth, she wished them back. Stupid to have pointed out she was suspended from work. "Look, Waylon, I have to go. Thanks again for the list. I owe you big time."

"It's okay, just stay safe," Waylon said.

"I will, thanks." She disconnected from the call, then wagged her fingers at Dallas's phone. "Has he texted the list yet?"

"No. David Cortney is the dead guy at the hotel?"

"Yes. The name means nothing to me," she admitted.

"Me either." Dallas sighed. "I have a computer, so I can try to do some digging, but that name isn't that unusual. Oh, here's the list of names and license plate numbers." He opened the text message and clicked on the attachment.

She crowded next to Dallas to scan the list of names. Of course, Cortney wasn't on there, so she assumed he'd either rented or stolen the car. "Wait a minute, don't you think the car was found at the hotel?"

"Hard to say since your cop friend didn't mention it."

"Yeah." She wished she'd thought to ask, but she wouldn't keep bothering Waylon. The poor kid would be in enough trouble already if her lieutenant found out about how he'd helped her.

Not that she planned to tell him. Fernando had been curt with her earlier, unwilling to give her anything other than they were still investigating. And reminding her that she was still off duty until further notice.

She missed having a badge, it would have been helpful to have if they ever found someone to question about Tate's murder. A scenario that wasn't looking likely.

"Hey, I found something," Dallas said, interrupting her thoughts.

"What?" He'd been studying the list of names and addresses associated with the license plates.

"Two of these cars have addresses in Austin, one of them close to the place where you told me Tate was living." He looked up from the phone. "When I drove by, there wasn't any crime scene tape across the door. I figured either Tate hadn't lived there recently or somehow the police haven't bothered to search it."

"Searching it should have been the first thing to do, right up there with creating a timeline of Tate's last-known activities." She frowned, trying to figure out what in the world her lieutenant was doing. Hard to believe he'd gone down the path of checking out her last movements in his efforts to treat her like a suspect rather than focusing on the dead man. "We need to check out all three of these Austin addresses."

"Something to think about for tomorrow, but the bigger

question is what about tonight?" He held her gaze for a long moment. "Do we stay, knowing the gunman could show up later? Or find somewhere else to go?"

A very good question. The car they'd seen driving past may not belong to the gunman. Even if it did, they had the cameras here, which would warn them of anyone getting too close. Not to mention Dallas's trip wires.

"I'm leaning toward staying," she finally said. "Especially after all the precautions you've taken." She hesitated, then added, "I feel my family is safe here with you, Dallas. More so than at a hotel."

"Our family," he corrected.

She stiffened, narrowing her gaze. "Don't push it. Just because Laney hasn't said much about her father's death doesn't mean she isn't thinking about it. It's a lot for an eight-year-old to process. Considering how she almost saw someone get gunned down earlier today, I'm not going to pile on more for her to deal with."

His jaw tensed, but he nodded. "I get that, but you need to start thinking about us differently. Your mother told me she knows I'm Laney's father, so she's aware of the situation too. Face it, I'm not going anywhere once the danger is over. The sooner you reconcile that, the better for everyone."

"Yes, you've made that very clear." She couldn't help being irritated by his comments. So much for him giving her time to come to grips with everything that has been going on. Tate's murder, gunmen coming for her, and his popping back into her life as if he'd never left her alone and pregnant. She tried to swallow her anger, but her tone was curt when she asked, "What about tonight? Are we staying or going?"

"We'll stay. Just make sure you're packed for a quick getaway if needed."

"Fine. Good night." She turned and hurried back to her bedroom. Maybe she was overreacting, but Dallas could be so maddening. One minute he was sweet and focused on protecting them, the next he was pressuring her to talk to Laney about how they were going to be one, big happy family.

Living happily ever after. At least until Dallas found some other woman he wanted to marry.

Then they'd be right back to fighting over a joint custody arrangement.

The depressing thought made it nearly impossible for her to fall asleep.

MENTALLY KICKING himself for upsetting Maggie, Dallas forced himself to stay focused on the threat. He moved from one room to the next, checking each window. They were all locked, the air was always cranked up in August, so there would be no reason to open them. Even at night, the temperature outside didn't drop much below eighty-five degrees.

He even sneaked into Laney's room to make sure her windows were locked. They were, and he stood for a moment watching his daughter sleep. She was so cute and peaceful he could have stood there all night.

It was still difficult to comprehend how he and Maggie had created such an amazing kid. One who loved to swim as much as he did.

He tore him gaze from her sweet face and returned to the main living space. Romeo stirred, but when Dallas stretched out on the sofa, he closed his eyes again. Dallas kept the phone close so the vibration would wake him if the car returned or a person tried to sneak up on the place.

If another gunman had been behind the wheel, he felt certain the guy would return sometime between three and four in the morning. It was a common time for the SEAL teams to deploy into dangerous territory. Their commanding officers used it because the body's biological rhythms were at their lowest point at that time, enabling them to sneak in easier, and of course, the cover of darkness always worked to their advantage.

He dozed while remaining alert to the sounds around him, a trick he'd learned as a SEAL. He woke himself up every hour. Each time he checked his phone to make sure he hadn't missed anything.

He hadn't. Yet his nerves were on edge waiting for the gunman to strike.

It occurred to him that he hadn't been this nervous when being sent into a terrorist cell. Maybe because he'd had his teammates covering his six.

The weight of keeping Laney, Sarah, and Mags safe weighed heavily on his shoulders. Maggie was armed, but the little girl and Maggie's mom were true innocents. They wouldn't react in a split second to a dangerous threat.

He decided he'd call Nico or Dawson in the morning, see if either of them would be willing to head to Texas to back him up. The reassuring thought helped him fall back to sleep.

His gut instincts woke him again at ten minutes before three o'clock in the morning. After checking the cameras on his phone, he rose and made another sweep around the interior of the house.

This time, Romeo stretched and joined him, tail wagging as if anticipating a training game. Normally he would hide scents for the dog to find, but not in the middle of the night.

The exterior of the house was quiet. No people, no cars. Romeo looked up at him expectantly, then sat in front of the garage door, indicating he wanted to go out.

He hesitated, then took him outside. While Romeo did his thing, he checked a few of the trip wires. They were still intact.

After bringing the dog inside, he spent the next hour pacing the house and watching his cameras.

The gunman didn't return.

By the time dawn broke over the horizon, he'd convinced himself the car that had driven by didn't belong to the gunman at all. He'd killed David Cortney, maybe there wasn't anyone else to come after them.

Doubtful, but possible. Regardless, he wasn't going to relax his guard. Laney would have to stay indoors again, except for swimming in the pool that was enclosed by screens to minimize the impact of the hot sun.

He thought about starting breakfast but settled for making a pot of coffee so he wouldn't wake the rest of the house. He took Romeo outside again, then thought about the information Mags had gotten from the rookie cop.

David Cortney and three Austin addresses belonging to car owners that met their partial plate description. He wanted to go check them out, especially the one closest to where Tate had lived, but that would mean leaving Maggie, Laney, and Sarah alone.

They'd been safe enough here yesterday, but that had been before the black car had gone past.

Twice.

He sipped his coffee, trying to come up with another avenue to get what he needed. The only way he'd feel comfortable leaving was if Nico, Dawson, or one of the other guys were here to keep an eye on the house while he was gone.

A plan he needed to discuss with Maggie.

Sarah came into the kitchen first, heading straight to the fridge. "I'll make breakfast," she announced.

"Are you sure?" He rose to join her. "I can make eggs too."

"I'm going a little stir-crazy here," she admitted. "I'd rather keep busy."

"Okay, thank you." He figured arguing would be pointless, besides, he could see that her features looked a bit strained. As if the recent events had robbed her of sleep.

Maggie came in next, looking better than ever. Her long, blond hair fell loosely around her shoulders, and her brown eyes were clear. He was glad she'd been able to get some rest. She poured herself a mug of coffee, then crossed over to the living room to look out the window. "Lots of traffic out there this morning," she observed.

"The locals going to work." He'd been alerted to the vehicles driving by, which could be a problem. Too many notifications lessened the importance of them.

Never a good thing.

"I'm going to call my SEAL buddies," he said in a low voice. "Nico is on Pacific time, so I'm going to wait another hour or so."

"Why? I'm a cop, there's no reason to drag others into this mess." She looked irritated. "I don't need your protection, Dallas. I can take care of myself."

"You're a great cop, but even cops have backup." He had to assume she was good at her job or she wouldn't have been promoted to detective. "It may take a day or two for them to get here anyway."

"Nice to know you have faith in my abilities." She turned away, but he caught her arm to stop her.

"I trust your ability, Mags," he said in a low voice. "I know you can protect yourself. But I've only just found out about Laney, so don't blame me for feeling overprotective of her."

Her scowl relaxed, and she nodded. "Fine, call them. But don't think I'm just going to sit by and wait for them to ride in to the rescue. I want to go check out those addresses. You can stay here with Laney and my mom."

It was his turn to frown. "Not a good idea when you're the target. I'm the one who needs to do the legwork. If I find something, you'll be the first to know."

"I can't sit here doing nothing, Dallas." She raked a hand through her hair. "I need to keep busy. To investigate."

"Once my backup arrives, we can work together." He couldn't squelch the surge of panic at her going off alone.

"Hi, Mom, Dallas. Romeo!" The chocolate lab rushed over to greet Laney with enthusiasm. "Did you miss me? Huh, boy? Did you?"

Watching Laney and Romeo together never failed to make him smile. They were rays of sunshine, spreading happiness wherever they went. It just made him that much more determined to keep them safe.

No matter what.

"Breakfast is ready," Sarah called.

He took a moment to feed Romeo, then joined them at the table. When Sarah sat down, Mags and Laney looked at him expectantly. He bowed his head and said grace. "Lord, we ask You to bless this food You have provided for us to eat. We ask that You guide us on Your chosen path. Amen."

"Amen," Sarah echoed. "That was nice, Dallas."

"Thanks." He shot her a quick look, wondering if she

really meant it or if there was a hint of sarcasm in her tone. It was only yesterday that she'd accused him of not protecting Maggie, but maybe she'd found a way to forgive him.

The way he needed to forgive himself.

He keenly regretted the position he'd put Maggie in, but he couldn't regret having Laney. All he could do now was make up for the time he'd lost with his daughter.

And with Maggie.

"Can I swim after breakfast?" Laney asked. "There's nothing else to do here."

He glanced at Maggie. "That's up to your mom."

"Sure, you can swim. But not until after we clean up the kitchen."

"I can do that," Sarah offered. "As Laney said, there's not much else to do here."

He could understand their feeling of restlessness, it wasn't easy to live in a strange house without all the stuff you normally took on a vacation. He quickly finished his meal and stood. "Come, Romeo."

"I want Romeo to swim with me," Laney protested.

"He will, but first I need to take him outside." He put the dog on leash to keep him from getting tangled in the trip wires.

The car that drove past last night bugged him. Were his instincts that off-kilter? He'd only been out of the navy for eight months, his gut shouldn't be rusty.

After all, he had been forced to kill a man yesterday.

He didn't think he'd lost his survival instincts, but maybe he had mistaken the simple drive-by for something sinister. While Romeo did his business, he swept the area for signs of trouble.

All was quiet.

Inside, he scoured the videos to see if the same car had returned. Finding nothing, he decided to head out to check the addresses.

"Stay and guard," he told Romeo.

The lab sat looking up at him expectantly. When Laney came out of her room dressed in a swimsuit, the dog's tail went crazy whipping back and forth in excitement.

"Go." He gestured to Laney. Romeo leaped up and ran after the little girl, following her outside and jumping into the pool.

He could feel Maggie's gaze on him as he headed out to the SUV. He felt bad for leaving her behind, but at the same time, he needed them to be safe. He backed out of the garage and headed toward the first address on his list, the one located near Tate Chandler's old place.

He took a meandering path, making sure he wasn't followed. There was no sign of the dark sedan from the night before. He sent up a prayer for God to protect his family as he navigated the streets of Austin.

Twenty minutes later, he drove past the address. The house appeared quiet, nobody was outside, and there wasn't a car in the driveway.

He decided to make a second pass, just to be sure. He was roughly a block away when the garage door rose, providing a glimpse of a black sedan. He kept driving, surreptitiously looking at the license plate.

TSV 722

It wasn't a match, despite what was listed on the sheet Waylon had provided. The male driver didn't seem to notice him. Dallas figured it couldn't hurt to follow the vehicle. If the guy was going to work or the grocery store, then he'd cross this one off his list and move on to the next.

He'd fully expected the car to head to some office building. But the driver took the closest highway. His pulse kicked up as he followed, keeping two cars between them.

Then the black sedan abruptly took the next exit, picking up speed. Dallas tried to keep up, but when he reached the intersection, the vehicle had vanished.

Clearly the driver had noticed his SUV and ditched him. Not something an innocent person would do. Had the license plate been switched to prevent the guy from being caught?

It was the first lead in the case, although one that wasn't much help. He was about to drive back to the guy's house to wait for him to return when he realized the black sedan could be heading for his house.

He hit the gas and sped back to the rental, hoping and praying he wasn't too late.

CHAPTER SEVEN

Maggie prowled around the house, peeking out the windows to make sure there was nothing amiss. She listened as Laney and Romeo played in the water, her mother sitting nearby to watch.

It bothered her to be left behind while Dallas was out attempting to uncover information about the case. Sure, he was a highly trained Navy SEAL, but she was the detective. Or she had been since it didn't look as if her boss would allow her to return to work anytime soon.

Sitting still was impossible, so she continued making rounds from one room to the next, checking every window. When she heard her phone buzzing, she frowned, worried Waylon had somehow given this number to the lieutenant. "Hello?"

"Maggie, be on the lookout for the black sedan, he may be heading to the rental house." Dallas's voice was tense. "I'm on my way."

She instantly moved to the open-concept living space overlooking the front street. "No sign of him yet. Did you get the license plate number?"

"Yeah, unfortunately it's not a match to the one on Waylon's list. I got a very clear look at it, though, and the driveway is the address that Waylon gave us. The current plate number is TSV seven two two."

She repeated the series of letters and numbers in her head, committing them to memory, then she tried to make sense of the information. "I don't understand why the plate is different if the address is correct."

"They may have switched license plates to throw us off the trail," Dallas said. "But I think it's more interesting that the driver noticed me following and managed to lose me. That's really suspicious."

"True, it also means the guy at the hotel must have had another ride, or the driver was waiting for him in the vehicle." She pulled her backup piece from her shoulder holster. "There's no sign of the black sedan yet. I'll get Laney and Romeo inside."

"Good idea. I'll be there as quickly as possible." He didn't wait for her to respond and disconnected from the call.

Maggie shoved her phone into her pocket and swept one more gaze up and down the street outside. Then she hurried over to open the patio doors. "Mom, Laney, time to come inside. Hurry."

"Aw, Mom," Laney protested. "We haven't been swimming that long."

"You can swim again later, but for now, get out of the water." Maggie kept her tone firm, and the nervous look from her mother indicated she was aware of the potential danger.

"Now, Laney," Sarah said. "Let's go."

"Okay," Laney said with a sigh.

Maggie turned back to watch the street in front of the

house. A car was coming from the west, and she tensed, positioning herself at the edge of the window. As it drew closer, she could see it was a dark blue rather than black.

Still, she didn't relax her guard. Maybe this wasn't the car Dallas had followed or he'd gotten the color wrong. The car drove past without stopping, but she continued watching the street, waiting for it to return. Behind her, the patio door opened, and Laney, her mother, and Romeo came inside.

She glanced over her shoulder. "Close the door and lock it."

Her mother did so, then asked, "What's going on?"

"Mom?" Laney asked, her eyes wide. "Is the bad guy coming back?"

"Nothing is going on, but I would feel better if you both went to your rooms for a bit. Just until Dallas gets back." She forced a smile. "I'm keeping an eye on things out here."

Laney's lower lip trembled. "I thought we would be safe . . ."

"We are," Maggie hastened to reassure her. "Trust me, okay? I won't let anything happen to you."

"Come, Laney, you need to get out of that swimsuit." Her mother wrapped her arm around the little girl's shoulders and led her down the hall to her room. Romeo looked between Laney and Maggie and instinctively came over to sit beside her.

"Good boy," she murmured, wincing as he brushed his wet fur against her legs. Peering through the window again, she noticed another car approaching from the same direction as the first one. Envisioning the streets of the subdivision in her mind, she knew the area was located northwest of Austin. The cars were coming in from the east, likely from the downtown area of the city

This time, the car was black. Everything inside Maggie went still as she watched it approach. If there was any sign of a gun, she'd shoot first and ask questions later.

A loud honking noise caught her off guard. What in the world? Romeo jumped up and began to bark as Dallas's familiar SUV came around the corner. The blare of the horn had the desired effect, the sedan lurched forward and disappeared around the corner.

No! He was getting away!

She yanked the front door open, then stopped as she saw Dallas waving her back inside. Romeo hovered at her side, clearly intending to protect her. She reluctantly stepped back, only to frown when Dallas pulled into the driveway.

"What are you doing? Go after him," she called.

"We need to get out of here," he said tersely. "Get your bags packed and grab whatever food you can. There's a small cooler we can use."

"But if you catch him . . ." She let her voice trail off because the stubborn expression on his face told her it was useless to argue.

And really, he was right to make Laney and her mom's safety a priority.

She went back inside and called out, "Mom? Laney? Grab your stuff. We need to go."

This time, there was no protest from either of them. Romeo stayed close at her side until Dallas came in, then the dog rushed toward him as if picking up on the dangerous situation.

"Hurry," he said tersely. "We don't have a lot of time."

She nodded and reached for her bag, which she'd already packed. Thankfully, her mother and Laney were also packed. Dallas pulled stuff out of the fridge, tossing items into the cooler.

Five minutes later, they were in the SUV. Dallas's expression was grim as they left the rental house behind.

"Where are we going?" Laney asked.

"Someplace new," Dallas said, finally drumming up a smile as he glanced back at Laney. "Don't worry, I've already asked for a house with a pool."

"When did you have time to arrange that?" she asked in a low voice.

"I have a friend securing the place for us," he admitted. "I didn't want it listed in either of our names."

The extra precaution made sense. The black car had found their current location somehow, and it seemed likely that the gunmen had traced Dallas's license plate to get his name and therefore had found the house he'd rented.

It didn't bode well for their current situation that the gunmen had the kind of connections that could track a person so thoroughly, though. It made her wonder all over again what Tate had gotten mixed up in.

And if her lieutenant was any closer to uncovering the truth about who'd killed him.

"How far away is it?" she asked.

"Not sure, he's going to get me the information soon."

She kept an eye on her passenger-side window for a tail. So far, there was no sign of the black sedan.

"A blue car drove by right before the black one," she said. "You're sure the vehicle you saw was black?"

"Yeah." He gestured to the phone sitting in the cupholder between them. "Scroll through the camera images."

She did so, using her thumb to go through the various

images of the cameras. "We should have brought them along," she said with a sigh.

A smile tugged at the corner of his mouth. "I bought extras the first time. We'll be able to use them at the new place."

"Smart man." She said the words lightly, but she was struck by how true they were. Buying extra supplies in case they'd have to move wasn't something she would have thought of. "You're always one step ahead, huh?"

He nodded. "Our training taught us to always be prepared for the worst-case scenario."

"Makes sense." And she was irked she hadn't thought of it herself. Seeing the black car that had driven past last night should have made her realize the threat was real.

Glancing back, she was glad to see Laney was preoccupied with her handheld video game. She met her mom's concerned gaze and nodded reassuringly before turning back to face the front. "Dallas, I don't really understand why the black car didn't come back last night, especially if they knew we were there."

"I've wondered that too," he agreed. "I think it's possible they were waiting for reinforcements."

She blinked. "Reinforcements?"

He shrugged. "It's the only thing that makes sense. I already took out one of their guys back at the hotel. The person in charge isn't going to risk losing more men, not without taking additional precautions."

"You're right," she whispered. "They were thinking it would be easy to take me out, but once you came into the picture, they needed to change their strategy."

"I think the drive-by last night and again today was to verify that we were in the same location. When I followed the car, he ditched me and probably thought it was safe to make another attempt against you. Thankfully, my getting there so quickly had him aborting that plan."

It made sense in a sick sort of way. "I wish there was a way to convince them I don't know anything."

"I wish so, too, but it's too late for that."

She glanced at him. "Because we killed their guy at the hotel."

"I did," he corrected. "But yeah. I'm sure that has changed things, and not for the better."

Before she could ask anything more, his phone rang. Rather than use the hands-free, he took the device and brought it to his ear. "Nico? What do you have for me?"

She remembered Nico was one of his teammates, the guy who lived on the West Coast and therefore was two hours behind of them.

"Okay, thanks. That sounds perfect. And don't worry about heading out there right away, follow up your lead first. If that doesn't pan out, then call me back."

At first Maggie hadn't wanted any help from Dallas's buddies, but it was clear they were floundering along in the dark. Without backup, they wouldn't be able to dig into whatever Tate had gotten himself involved in. They were flying blind without understanding who was coming after them or why.

All they had was a whole lot of speculation without one shred of proof.

DALLAS QUICKLY MEMORIZED the address of the new place Nico had secured for them. It sounded crazy expensive, but his request had been specifically for a place with a pool and without any neighbors.

Nico had found a nice property for rent overlooking Lake Buchanan. The place sat on a full acre of land, and the nearest house next to them sat on a larger piece of land. He'd still use the extra cameras he'd purchased. The difference being that any car, motorcycle, bicycle, or person coming anywhere close to the house would be treated as suspicious.

He wasn't going to risk being found again.

"How long will it take to get there?" Laney asked.

Dallas caught her gaze in the rearview mirror. "Less than an hour. Try not to worry, okay? You're going to like the new place we're going to."

"I am?" Laney brightened. "Because of the pool?"

"The pool and there's a lake too. But you can't go to the lake without an adult."

"Sounds awesome," Laney said.

"I hope you like it." He was secretly amazed at how well she was handling all of this. Maybe being exposed to police work through her mom had made her grow somewhat accustomed to the danger.

"Lake Buchanan?" Mags echoed. "Isn't that a pricey place?"

"I've never been there, but Nico scoped it out and felt the place will work well for our needs." He didn't bother to add that he trusted his buddy implicitly. He knew that once Nico had talked to Jill, one of Ava's friends, to find out what if anything she knew about where Jaydon's sister may be hiding out, his buddy would call and be on the first flight out of LA, heading to Austin to join him.

Dallas welcomed having some backup. He'd tried Dawson, too, but he was on his honeymoon. He was surprised at how the guys had started getting married; four of them had now tied the knot. Leaving only Dallas and Nico single.

The thought made him glance at Maggie. Nine years ago, he was prepared to marry her. Only to discover she'd already married another man. In the years since, he'd never been tempted by another woman. Maggie had been the only woman he'd loved.

She was different now, though. Partially because she was a mother. Also because she was a detective. He'd been impressed with her being a cop nine years ago, but now he couldn't help but wonder if their relationship would have stood the test of time. He wanted to believe it would have, but then again, being married to a SEAL wasn't easy.

There was no point in thinking about what might have been. The way Maggie was keenly watching the traffic around them forced him to do the same. So far, he hadn't noticed anyone following, but the truth was, if the gunman had brought in additional reinforcements, they could be driving anything.

Better to stay focused on every car around them just in case.

He headed north for a bit, then turned west. When he found a smaller, less-traveled road, he took that, noting with satisfaction that not one single car followed them on the rural road.

He decided to make a loop before heading back down to the general area where Lake Buchanan was located. The property had been rented under Nico's name, which should ensure their anonymity.

"I'm bored," Laney complained.

"Let's watch a movie," Sarah said. "I have headphones here and Dallas's tablet. What would you like to watch?"

The two put on earphones and soon were watching a

show. He was relieved that he and Maggie could talk more freely now.

"At some point, I should call my boss again," Maggie said with a sigh. "Maybe I can convince him to share some information."

"Try him now," he advised. "And use your disposable phone, just in case."

She nodded and made the call. "Lieutenant Fernando, please. Yes, you can tell him this is Detective Chandler."

Dallas could only hear her part of the conversation. And it seemed her boss was doing most of the talking.

"I know I should have told you about the gunman at the hotel," she said. "But you need to know he was shot in self-defense. We couldn't stay, not knowing Laney was in danger. What I need to know is if you've tied him to Tate's murder."

Another long silence as she listened.

"I can't do that because my family is in danger. If there's anything you know that can help keep us safe, I'm all ears. There isn't enough manpower within our department to keep watch over us twenty-four seven." After another few seconds, she blew out a sigh of frustration. "Fine, I'll check back with you tomorrow."

"What did he say?" Dallas asked.

"They don't have me listed as their prime suspect anymore, but I'm still not cleared to work the investigation. The gun they took off the guy at the hotel had the serial number removed."

"Illegal weapons," he murmured. "Your ex may have gotten himself tangled up in selling them."

"Anything is possible," she admitted. Then she reached over to touch his arm. "You know, years ago, when Tate and I were still patrol officers, there was a complaint from some guy who said he had four guns when he was pulled over, but only one was turned into evidence."

He arched a brow. "And your ex is the one who pulled him over?"

She nodded. "To be honest, the guy had a long arrest history, so nobody took his claim very seriously. But now it makes me wonder if Tate had helped himself to the guns."

"Three guns doesn't mean much, though," he argued. "The illegal arms business sells hundreds of guns each month."

"True, but this was also over four years ago," she said, glancing over her shoulder to make sure her mother and Laney were still wearing headphones. "Many criminals start small before moving up into bigger and better things."

She made a good point, it was easy to imagine a guy like her ex getting greedy after getting away with making easy money. He considered the little bit she'd told him about Tate Chandler. "Did he leave the force soon after the complaint was filed?"

"Maybe six months later," she said. "Our marriage was rocky at that point anyway, so I wasn't really paying that much attention. Tate was coming and going at odd hours, and since I'd already caught him cheating, I never asked where he was."

"Cheating?" He scowled. "That's just wrong."

She shrugged. "Yeah, well, it doesn't matter anymore. But it does make me wonder about this so-called rich guy he went to work for. Maybe that guy is the brains behind the illegal guns."

"You don't remember his name?"

"No. I was happy Tate was moving out, so I didn't ask. Although, like I said, he did have his own place for the first couple of years. I dropped Laney off there." She put a hand over her stomach. "It makes me sick to think he may have put our daughter in danger back then. And it also explains why he stopped making time for her." She scowled. "Maybe he did grow a conscience along the way."

"Then why would he ask to have full custody?"

"I have no idea." She stared out the window for a bit, then glanced back to check behind them. Thankfully, there were no other cars on this rural road. "I don't think he really wanted custody, though. I think the call was some sort of weird message."

"Like code?"

"No, he wasn't that smart." She winced, then said, "Sorry, that was uncalled for."

His opinion of Tate Chandler had the guy lower than a snake, but he didn't say it. "What did he say when you mentioned going to your lawyer?"

"Just that he'd do the same." Then her hand shot out to grab his arm. "No, wait. What he said was something like you'll get a package from me. I told him to send it to my lawyer, and he just laughed and said it was already on its way."

His heart thudded against his chest. "A package? What kind of package?"

"I don't know." Her fingers tightened. "Maybe it was some sort of code. Like he was using the custody arrangement as an excuse to send me something. We need to head back to my place, Dallas. We need to see if a package was delivered and what it contains. Maybe Tate was trying to get away from these guys."

He had to admit it was a strong possibility. "Okay, but we can't do that now. First, we need to get to the new safe house."

"No, we need to detour to Fredericksburg right away,"

she insisted. "We need to find that package before the bad guys do."

He didn't like it, but he could see her point. There had to be another way to get the job done. "Do you trust Waylon to check your place?"

She hesitated, then shook her head. "I trust him, but I can't keep asking him to do things for me. He'll get in trouble. The mail carrier usually hits our place between eleven and noon, so we have time to get over there before the package is dropped off."

"Unless it was delivered yesterday," he argued. "We don't know if he used the US mail service or another company, like UPS or FedEx."

"I guess he may have, but if he was buying time, he'd use the regular mail. The mail delivery out here is notoriously slow. We didn't get a package the day Tate was killed, and that was probably the day he mailed it. So it's not likely it would have gotten there by yesterday. Today's the day, Dallas. I'm certain of it." Her brown eyes caught his. "The package could be what we need to get to the bottom of this mess."

He swallowed a groan. "Okay, fine. We'll head back to Fredericksburg." He didn't love the idea of going back to where this had all started. Logically, he had to believe the bad guys knew about the package, otherwise why come after Maggie in the first place? And if they did, they'd no doubt have someone stationed nearby watching the place for the delivery, with orders to intercept the package.

He was confident in his ability to get in and out of Maggie's house without being seen, moving stealthily was something the SEALs excelled at.

The bigger question was how to keep Maggie, Laney, and Sarah safe while he was gone. Having them in the safe house would have been the better option, but it would take too long. He didn't dare miss the mail delivery.

The only plan he could come up with was to ask his sister, Brenda, to help. The three of them could hang out with Brenda at the tourist shop while he borrowed his sister's car to get to Maggie's place.

Putting Brenda and Jason in danger didn't sit well with him. Yet Brenda's last name was Jones, so hopefully whoever hired the gunmen didn't know anything about his sister or his nephew.

He quickly turned at the next intersection to head back toward Highway 16, his usual route of getting to Fredericksburg from the north side of Austin. Ironic to realize it was less than forty-eight hours since he'd taken that same path to his sister's only to run into Maggie.

Which had then brought him to his daughter.

Clearly God had sent him down this path for a reason. To find Maggie and Laney in time to keep them safe from harm. He sent up a silent prayer, asking the Lord for wisdom and guidance.

He couldn't do this alone, not without God's help.

After about fifteen minutes of driving, Laney removed her earbuds. "Hey, this doesn't look like the lake."

"You're right, it's not. We need to go to Fredericksburg for a few minutes," Maggie told her.

"That will take too long," Laney whined. "You said the new place has a pool, and I wanna swim and play with Romeo."

"You've had lots of swimming time," Maggie said firmly. "I'm sure there will be plenty of time once we get to the house."

Dallas wisely kept his mouth shut. The detour to Fredericksburg and back to Lake Buchanan would take them almost three hours.

But if they were able to get the package, and it contained the proof they needed to understand what was going on, the trip would be well worth it.

CHAPTER EIGHT

The drive into Fredericksburg seemed to take forever. Maggie's nerves were on edge, her mind whirling as she thought about the package Tate had sent. Or that she hoped he'd sent. There was the possibility that being murdered had prevented him from doing so.

She swallowed hard and tried to remain positive. There had to be a reason the gunman kept coming after her. All this time she'd felt certain it was related to her brief conversation with Tate, that they'd assumed he'd told her something he shouldn't have.

It occurred to her that she should let Fernando know about the package. Certainly, whatever was enclosed would be crucial to Tate's homicide investigation. But she wanted to see what it was first. For all they knew, it could be nothing more than legal paperwork challenging their co-custody agreement.

But she didn't think so. No, the whole phone call had been so strange in the first place she was mentally kicking herself for not picking up on the undertone of Tate's comments earlier. If she had figured it out right away—maybe he'd still be alive.

Some detective she'd turned out to be.

With an effort, she forced herself to concentrate on watching for a tail. Nothing had caught her eye so far, but that didn't mean much. She was second-guessing everything now.

Especially her own instincts.

"How long is this gonna take?" Laney asked. "I'm bored."

Suppressing a sigh, she turned to look at her daughter. "It won't be that long, and maybe we can grab something for lunch on the way back to Lake Buchanan. You love tacos, right? We'll swing by Mateo's Tacos."

The bribe worked. "Yeah! Tacos! Extra hot, right, Mom?"

"The way you like them," she agreed.

"Extra hot, huh?" Dallas drawled. "Sounds like a challenge."

Laney grinned and nodded. "The hotter the better."

Maggie eyed Dallas, impressed with his ability to lighten the situation. For a guy who didn't have kids—well, other than Laney—he was doing a good job of managing things. Which was both encouraging and depressing.

No, she would not be selfish about Dallas's role in Laney's life. Her mother was right when she pointed out that Laney deserved to have a father who loved and cared for her. In a way Tate had never done.

Which meant she needed to tell Laney the truth about Dallas, sooner rather than later. The little girl hadn't said much about Tate's death and would be absolutely thrilled about learning her real dad was alive and well.

Tonight, she silently promised. They would have that conversation tonight. Hopefully, the danger would be mitigated by then.

The banter over hot tacos continued as they approached Fredericksburg. She glanced at Dallas as he headed through town, bypassing the way to her place.

"We're going to stop and visit my sister," he said, reading the unspoken question in her eyes. "I'm going to borrow her car while you guys hang out at the shop."

She knew he was planning to head to her place alone. It was frustrating to leave the investigation in his hands, but she couldn't deny he had a better chance of getting in and out without being seen, especially if someone was keeping watch.

And she couldn't suppress a sense of unease at being back in Fredericksburg. It wasn't that long ago that they'd been found at the hotel by the gunman. She needed to protect Laney and her mom long enough for Dallas to get in and out of her place.

Praying that they hadn't already missed the package delivery.

When Dallas parked his SUV a block away from the shop, she subtly passed him her house keys, then glanced back at her mom. "Ready?"

"Of course." Her mother's smile was strained, and Maggie felt bad for dragging her mother through all of this. But it was better than the alternative.

"What about Romeo?" Laney asked. "Does he get to stay with us?"

Dallas hesitated, then nodded as he stuffed the keys into his pocket. "I would appreciate you watching over Romeo while I'm gone."

"Goody," Laney said with a smile, apparently not understanding the seriousness of the situation. "I'll take him for a long walk."

"I'm afraid he'll have to stay with us at the tourist shop," Maggie said.

"Brenda has an apartment up above the tourist shop," Dallas said. "Y'all can stay up there for a while. I won't be long."

"Aw, do we havta?" Laney sighed dramatically. "We've been sitting in the car forever."

"Laney," Maggie warned. "Enough."

Her daughter sighed, but thankfully she stopped complaining. Dallas slid out from behind the wheel, freed Romeo from the back, then walked around to help Laney and her mom out.

He handed Romeo's leash to Laney, pinning her with a serious look. "Take good care of him while I'm gone."

"I will." Laney rested her hand on Romeo's head. "I love him."

"Good." Dallas ushered them down the block toward the tourist gift shop his sister owned and operated. When they all crowded inside, Brenda glanced up in surprise. "Dallas. I—uh, wasn't expecting y'all."

"I know, sorry about that." Dallas moved closer to where she stood behind the counter. "I need to borrow your car for a short while, and I'd like Laney, Sarah, and Maggie to hang out upstairs while I'm gone."

Brenda's eyes widened. "What's going on?"

"Nothing you need to worry about," he hastened to reassure her. "Where's Jason?"

His sister shrugged. "Working, or so he claims. He left earlier this morning."

Dallas nodded. "Okay, that's good. I'll fill you in later, but for now, I need to get moving. And I really need to borrow your car."

"Fine with me." Brenda didn't hesitate to hand over her car keys. Dallas didn't linger and quickly left the shop.

"I'm sorry he dumped us on you without warning," Maggie said apologetically. Two adults, a child, and a dog took up most of the room in the small shop. "Is there something we can do to help you?"

"No, it's fine." Brenda moved out from behind the counter. "Follow me, my apartment is upstairs."

"Thanks for doing this," Maggie murmured.

Brenda didn't say anything as they followed her up to the apartment. It was warm thanks to the sun streaming in through the eastern-facing windows. "Uh, sorry, it's not very big."

"It's fine," Maggie assured her. "I'm sorry to put you out."

"Come, Romeo," Laney said, heading over to the sofa. Romeo bounded after her.

Brenda's gaze tracked the little girl, and Maggie knew what she was thinking. There hadn't been a lot of time to think about how Dallas had learned about Laney, but she suspected Brenda had told him about her pregnancy.

"I'll be downstairs if you need anything," Brenda said, turning toward the door.

Maggie followed her down the stairs and into the shop. "Brenda, Dallas knows the truth about Laney."

She winced. "Because I told him you were pregnant when you got married."

"I know, and it's okay. The only issue is that we haven't had time to explain things to Laney yet, so if you could keep the news quiet a little longer, I'd appreciate it."

"You're not mad at me?" Brenda asked.

"Not at all." Truthfully, she had been upset at Dallas finding out, but that had been a knee-jerk reaction. This was about what was best for Laney. "I'm grateful for Dallas's help these past few days."

"What's going on?" Brenda asked. "I heard there have been two homicides. Everyone is looking over their shoulder, fearing for their safety." She frowned, then added, "I thought you'd be investigating what happened."

"I wish I was, but it's a long story, and honestly, the less you know, the better." The tinkle of a bell announced a new shopper. "Take care, we'll be out of your hair as soon as possible."

Brenda frowned but didn't argue. Instead, she hurried over to greet the newcomer. "Hi, my name is Brenda. Is there anything in particular y'all are looking for today?"

Maggie headed back upstairs. She could hear by the tense discussion between Laney and her mother that the next hour of sitting around doing nothing wouldn't be fun.

"Laney, you need to stop, right now." She narrowed her gaze. "Dallas asked us to be patient, so we need to make the best of the situation. Why not play the video game Nanna brought you?"

"Okay," Laney groused. She took the video game and sat back on the sofa, looking irritated. Romeo jumped up beside her, which brought a reluctant smile to her daughter's face.

Crisis averted for the moment. But as the minutes passed with excruciating slowness, all Maggie could think about was Dallas.

She found herself murmuring a small prayer, asking for God to keep Dallas safe and to grant him the ability to retrieve the package Tate had sent.

Please, Lord, we dearly need Your strength and support!

DALLAS PARKED Brenda's white Toyota Camry four blocks from Maggie's house. He slid from the vehicle, locking the doors and pocketing the key.

Easier to sneak into a place in the darkness, but he wasn't going to let the hot sun beating down prevent him from getting the job done. Thankfully, he'd walked the perimeter of Maggie's property twice in the short time he'd been there.

The hardest part would be making his way through the quiet neighborhood without raising an alarm. He planned to take a shortcut through various properties to reach the back of Maggie's house. If anyone was outside watching the place, he felt certain they'd be somewhere out front where they would have a clear view of the front door and the approach of a mail carrier or delivery truck. The intense heat may work in his favor, as it was common for the locals to close the blinds against the sun during the hottest part of the day.

He had driven past the houses on this block before choosing a place to park, picking the light green house as his target. The dilapidated exterior made him think the owner either didn't get out much or didn't care enough to tidy things up. One side window even had newspaper taped over it.

That was the side of the house he quickly approached, moving slowly and deliberately, hoping to avoid drawing attention.

He made it through that property and the next before crouching behind a small shed. He took a moment to glance around in case someone had come out to investigate.

Thankfully, he didn't see anyone. The neighborhood was quiet, and he wondered how that worked out for Laney. She'd mentioned swimming with her friend Jane, but it didn't appear there were a lot of other kids her age living nearby.

That was a consideration for another day. He remained crouched near the shed for a full five minutes before moving through the next property.

From here, he could see the back of Maggie's house. He pulled the keys from his pocket, then made the final trip to her back door. There were four keys on the ring, but the second one unlocked the door. He gratefully slipped inside, softly closing the door behind him.

The first part of his plan had worked fine. But he knew the danger wasn't over. If there was someone outside watching, they likely had binoculars. Thankfully, there were blinds over some of the windows, and he quickly moved through the interior to the front living space, staying away from the few windows that weren't covered.

A couple of small letter-sized envelopes were lying on the floor below the mail slot in the front door. No package or large envelope, but he went over to double-check anyway. Junk mail and one credit card bill. He wondered why she didn't just use the online version before realizing the bill was addressed to Sarah not Maggie.

The house was likely in Sarah's name. He slowly straightened, trying to think of a way to reach the mail carrier before he got to the house.

He edged to the main window overlooking the street and peered out cautiously. To his surprise, there wasn't a vehicle within sight.

Either no one was watching the place or they were parked well outside of his line of sight.

Dallas swiftly moved toward the master suite. Barely moving the blinds, he managed to see further down the street.

Still no vehicles nearby.

He checked from Maggie's room, too, with the same result. But the news didn't help him relax. Instead, he worried he was missing something.

These guys had tracked Maggie's phone or found his name through his DMV records. They had to be keeping an eye on the place.

He made rounds again at all the windows, this time carefully examining the properties nearby. The one across the street caught his interest. The front blinds weren't drawn, and he felt certain they had been two days ago.

He pulled out his phone to call Maggie.

"Did you find it?" she asked.

"Not yet. Tell me about your neighbors."

"The house to the east is owned by an elderly couple who head north during the hot summer months. They have a son who lives in Springfield, Missouri, and they claim it's not as hot there. The house to the west is owned by a single woman who works long hours."

"What about the place directly across the street?"

"That is a rental property, but it's often vacant during the summer. Not many people come to stay during July and August."

Bingo, he thought. "Okay, thanks." He disconnected from the line and returned to the master suite. He wasn't sure which direction the mail carrier would come in from, so he'd have to go back and forth between the rooms to watch for him.

The hour crept past eleven. He went from window to window every four minutes, taking the occasional stop near the front to check the house across the street. He caught a glimpse of movement near the window and felt certain there was someone inside waiting and watching.

The same way he was.

At eleven thirty-three, he caught a glimpse of the mail carrier's truck from the master suite window. Without hesitation, he left Maggie's place through the back door, taking precious seconds to lock up, then ducked through the next two backyards heading east.

He didn't want to scare the mail carrier, but he couldn't risk the watcher across the street reaching him first either. God was guiding him because he managed to catch the guy as he was riffling through the mail inside the side door of his truck. The angle was just enough to keep the watcher across the street from seeing them.

He hoped.

"Excuse me," he said to the postal carrier. "I need to grab Sarah Stevenson's and Maggie Chandler's mail."

The carrier scowled. "Can't do that. Gotta deliver it to the proper address, and y'all don't look like Sarah or Maggie."

True enough. He pulled out his phone again and dialed Maggie. "Will you please speak to the mail carrier? He doesn't want to give me your mail."

"Sure," she replied.

He handed the guy the phone. The carrier eyed him suspiciously as he spoke into the phone. "Detective Chandler? Is that really you?" There was a slight pause, then he said, "Y'all are in danger?"

Dallas felt the back of his neck prickle with fear as the mail carrier took his sweet time verifying that, yes, it was okay for him to give Dallas her mail. He kept his eye on the street toward the west, half expecting men with guns to show up any second.

Finally, the carrier handed him the phone back. "This is highly unusual," he groused as he rummaged through his stack of mail. "I have a system and handing mail out to a stranger isn't right. I could lose my job over this."

"I know, and I wouldn't ask if it wasn't a matter of life and death." It took all Dallas's willpower to wait patiently for the guy to flip through items before turning to hand him the small stack of mail. His pulse kicked up when he saw a large, plain brown envelope with Maggie's name on it.

He took the items from the carrier's outstretched hand. "Thank you so much."

"You're welcome."

Dallas didn't linger but quickly turned. He decided to walk farther away from Maggie's house before ducking around to cut through several yards to get back to the vehicle.

By the time he reached the street where he'd left Brenda's car, he was running toward it. He jumped in behind the wheel and took off, hoping and praying that the watcher across the street wouldn't come after him.

He didn't breathe easy until he returned to Brenda's store. He'd taken as many detours as he could to avoid being followed. Yet just knowing Maggie's house was being watched had his nerves on edge.

"You're back," Brenda said when he entered the store.

"Thanks again for letting me use your car." He dropped the keys next to the register. "Everything okay here? No problems?"

"Everything is fine, although I get the impression Laney

is bored out of her mind." She searched his gaze. "She's really your daughter?"

"Yeah. And I owe you a debt of gratitude for cluing me in about Maggie's pregnancy and rushed marriage." His smile faded as he gestured toward the stairs. "I'm sorry to pop in and out like this, but we need to hit the road. I promise you'll get the full story sometime soon, okay?"

"I'm going to hold you to that promise," she teased. "Go ahead, I'm sure they're ready to get out of here too."

"Thanks again." He was somewhat surprised Brenda was more interested in Laney than in the way he'd borrowed her car. He stepped around the register, gave her a quick hug, then headed upstairs. The minute he reached the top, Maggie and Romeo were waiting.

"You found it." Maggie's gaze had instantly landed on the large envelope.

"Yep. Come on, we need to hit the road." He glanced over at Laney. "I promised you lunch at Mateo's."

"Finally!" Laney jumped off the sofa. "I'm starving."

Maggie didn't move but reached over to grab the envelope from the stack of mail in his hands. "We need to look at this first," she insisted. "If it's what we think it is, we'll have to turn it over to the police."

The urge to get out of town was strong, but he reluctantly nodded. He handed the rest of the mail to Sarah while Maggie opened the envelope. She pulled out a stack of what looked to his eye to be legal paperwork.

"I don't understand," she muttered, staring at the top page.

He stepped closer to read over her shoulder. "It looks like something his lawyer drafted."

"I know, but . . ." She frowned and paged through the stack. She got halfway through when she suddenly stopped and pulled a page out from the others. "This is it," she whispered.

"Show me."

She took a moment to read through the wording on the page before wordlessly handing it over to him. The way she looked over at Laney made him realize she didn't want to discuss their find out loud for her to hear.

The single sheet of paper described the process of selling and distributing ghost guns, which were basically homemade guns that were put together in pieces that could be purchased separately and put together to make an untraceable weapon. No serial number and no background checks required.

He didn't have much experience with the term, other than the US government had recently passed legislation to curb the use of ghost guns. Making it harder to sell and distribute the individual parts.

Yet where there was a will, there was a way. And criminals in general preferred using these untraceable weapons.

At the end of the paragraph, there was a website called We've Got Your Back. He had to assume the website owner was running a ghost gun operation. It sounded as if he may be targeting criminals to sell them these kits.

Why Tate had decided to get out of the business, he wasn't sure. Unless Tate had known things were going bad. It made him angry that Tate had put Maggie in harm's way. Except the truth was, if the gunman hadn't come after her, she would have gotten this information and taken it straight to the authorities.

"Okay, let's go." He handed the sheet of paper back to her. Rather than tucking it back into the envelope, she folded it and slid it into her pocket. He thought that was a smart move, being prepared in case someone tried to snatch it away. "We'll discuss our next steps on the way."

"We can't keep this to ourselves," Maggie protested.

"I know. But let's get to a safe place first, then worry about the rest." The itch along the back of his neck had returned.

He wanted to get out of Fredericksburg ASAP.

CHAPTER NINE

Ghost guns. That topic hadn't been anywhere close to what Maggie had expected to find. In their small town of Fredericksburg, she hadn't even seen a ghost gun, although she had been aware of their existence.

While she was glad to have something to go on, she was mad at Tate all over again.

Rather than going to the authorities, he'd sent the information to her, hidden within legal documents. Way to drag her into his mess. And okay, she was a cop and fully capable of protecting herself, something Tate had probably known.

But what about Laney? And her mom?

Just more proof that Tate had never truly considered Laney his daughter. How that was possible when he'd spent the first few years of her life with her, she had no clue. Glancing at Dallas's grim expression, she knew it was something he never would have done.

Even if Laney hadn't been his daughter biologically, he was the type of man who would put his life on the line to protect any child. Hadn't he dedicated his life to serving his country? Quite the opposite of how Tate had taken a darker path.

One that had gotten him ruthlessly murdered.

"Follow me back to the SUV," Dallas said. "Let's stay quiet too, okay?"

Laney looked scared but nodded. Romeo stayed right at her daughter's side as they headed down the stairs to the tourist shop.

Instead of going out through the front door, though, Dallas took the rear door. The hot August heat blasted their faces as they stepped outside. They'd left the SUV a few blocks down, and Dallas swept his gaze right and left as they walked toward it.

Maggie clutched the envelope to her chest, keeping a keen eye out for anything suspicious too. Sweat pooled in the hollow of her neck, making her wish she'd pulled her hair back into its usual ponytail. That's what happened when you allowed vanity to mess with your head. Stupid idea to try to look nice for Dallas.

They reached the SUV without issue. While Dallas put Romeo in the back, she made sure her mother and Laney were settled too. Soon, they were on their way.

"Are we still getting tacos from Mateo's?" Laney asked, trepidation underscoring her tone.

The restaurant was on the main thoroughfare through town. Maggie glanced at Dallas who gave a slight shake of his head, then turned to look at her daughter. "I think we'll have to wait a bit, sorry. But we'll find something to eat soon, okay?"

Laney's lower lip quivered. "A-are we in danger again?"

Her mother put a reassuring hand on Laney's arm. Maggie managed a smile, wishing she could hug the little girl. "We're safe, and nothing is going to happen to you. We would just like to get to the new house as soon as possible. You're still interested in swimming, right?"

Even the mention of her favorite pastime didn't cheer Laney up. "I guess."

"I know Romeo would like to swim," Dallas added. "I think there's a burger place just a few miles from here. We'll use the drive-through to grab lunch."

"I don't wanna burger," Laney whined.

"Chicken bites, then," Maggie said, giving her a stern look. "I know you like them, and this isn't the time to be picky."

"Fine. I'll have chicken bites," Laney said with a huff.

"Good." She turned back to face forward. The corner of Dallas's mouth tipped up in a smile.

"Nicely done," he murmured.

"Lots of practice." She noticed he was making several turns through town before heading to the highway. "I'd like to call my boss soon."

"Wait until we're at Lake Buchanan," he said. "It's not like we have a lot to tell him other than the website information."

She glanced at his phone in the cupholder. "Unlock your phone, I want to check out that website."

He hesitated, picked up the device, and unlocked it. She took it and put the website information into the browser.

It didn't come up.

Frowning, she tried again, being careful to type it in correctly.

Still nothing. She closed her eyes and swallowed a groan.

"What?" Dallas asked.

"It's already been taken down." She set the phone back

SEALED WITH TRUST   127

in the cupholder. "They must have suspected Tate gave me the information."

"Is there a tech expert within your police department?"

She shrugged. "Kent Simmons knows some tech stuff, but if you're asking if he can recreate it, I highly doubt it."

"Maybe we need to talk to someone within ATF," Dallas said. "I'm sure they'd be interested in getting to the bottom of this."

"That's a good idea," she agreed. The Alcohol, Tobacco, Firearms and Explosives branch of the federal government focused most of their time and efforts on tracking illegal guns and bombs. "I don't know anyone who works there, do you?"

"No, and I'm not sure your average citizen can call them directly." He shrugged. "We can check their website or ask your boss to contact them. I'm sure they have plenty of agents throughout the state of Texas."

She nodded, knowing he was right. As a government entity, they were spread across the entire US. It made her feel better to have an action plan. Although she wasn't sure her boss would be willing to contact the feds. She'd have to lean on him a bit. After all, this situation had already resulted in two deaths.

Maybe others, too, that they weren't even aware of.

Besides, most of the illegal activity hadn't taken place in Fredericksburg, more likely in Austin and maybe even other big cities nearby, like Waco.

Well outside their jurisdiction.

Dallas finally hit the highway. A short time later, he pulled into the drive-through lane of a fast-food restaurant.

"I know Laney is getting chicken bites, but what about you, Sarah? And Maggie?"

They provided their meal orders, and Dallas added his

too. He paid, then handed the bag to her. "We'll eat on the way."

"I hope you don't mind crumbs in the car," she warned, handing the food out.

"Nah, that's one area where Romeo comes in handy."

"I thought he couldn't eat people food," Laney protested.

"That's true, don't give him any of yours," Dallas warned. "But licking up crumbs is fine, he won't get sick from that."

"Okay, I don't want him to get sick either," Laney agreed.

Maggie handed Dallas his burger, then realized they needed to pray. She glanced back at her mother, who normally led their prayers at home, especially after losing her pastor husband. Her mother nodded encouragingly for Maggie to take the lead, so she bowed her head. "Lord, we ask You to bless this food we are about to eat. Amen."

"Amen," Dallas, her mother, and Laney echoed.

She ate quickly, then caught Laney licking her fingers, patting the chicken bites to get crumbs on them, then pressing her fingers through the crate for Romeo. "Enough, Laney. Eat your food."

"But it's only crumbs," Laney said.

She noticed Dallas wryly shook his head. "Figures," he murmured. "I should have known better." Then he raised his voice louder. "Your mother is right, Laney. Time for you to finish your meal."

Yes, he should have known better, give a kid an inch, and they'll take a mile. But she was glad he didn't become angry or upset. She sensed it would take a lot for him to lose his temper with Laney.

The drive to Lake Buchanan seemed to take forever,

although part of that was getting off the main highway and using rural roads to reach their destination. She had to admit the area was beautiful. There were more hills and valleys, and soon she caught a glimpse of the shimmering lake.

"Can we swim in the lake this afternoon?" Laney asked, craning her head to see out the window. "It looks huge."

"Not today," Dallas said. "But wait until you see the pool. It's bigger than the one at the other house."

"Bigger?" Laney's brown eyes gleamed. "Cool!"

Maggie felt her jaw drop in shock when they reached the rental property. It was huge and must have cost Dallas three times as much or more than the previous place. "Looks like we're living the life of the rich and famous."

He flashed a smile. "It wasn't easy to find something that matched my specific criteria of having a pool and no close neighbors."

No kidding. Still, she was glad there weren't any houses nearby. She could see one place about two hundred yards away, but that was about it.

They unpacked the car, including the cooler. Their detour into Fredericksburg had caused the ice packs inside to melt, but thankfully, the food hadn't spoiled.

"I'm ready to swim," Laney announced. She ran into the living room wearing her swimsuit. "I can't find the ball, though."

"I have it." Dallas rummaged in a bag and produced a bright orange ball. He tossed it up into the air, and Romeo leaped up to snag it. "You need to promise me you'll stay in the pool area, okay?"

"I promise. Come, Romeo." Laney pulled the patio doors open and took the chocolate lab outside.

"I'll watch them," Sarah offered.

"Thanks, Mom." Maggie finished unpacking, then took a moment to look around the layout of the house. It was a sprawling ranch with four bedrooms, two and a half bathrooms, and a wonderful view of Lake Buchanan. The pool and patio weren't enclosed like the last property, which made her a bit nervous.

Then again, the lack of neighbors helped.

"I'll put up cameras," Dallas said as if reading her mind. "And trip wires too."

"I know." She managed a smile. "It's really an incredible piece of property."

"Yep. And ours for the next two weeks."

"Two weeks? This must get wrapped up before then."

He nodded. "I hope so, too, but that's how much is paid for in advance." He hesitated, then added, "Maybe once the threat has been neutralized, we can stay a few extra days on a mini-vacation."

"Maybe." She understood what he really wanted was to spend time with Laney as a family. "We'll talk to her tonight, Dallas. But right now, we need to call my boss and the ATF."

"Tonight?" He visibly brightened. "Really? You mean that?"

"Yes. It's clear Laney isn't grieving over losing her father, Tate." She sighed and smiled. "I'm sure she'll be thrilled to learn she has a dad in you."

"I hope so." Dallas looked a bit uncertain. "I want to be there for her, and for you too. I'm sure being a single parent hasn't been easy."

"Not easy, but I've been blessed to have my mom helping me." She glanced out to where her mother was sitting in a chair, watching Laney and Romeo jumping in and out of the water. "It's been good for both of us, really, since my dad died."

"How long ago did you lose him?" Dallas's light green eyes were sympathetic.

"Five years ago now. Three years after . . ." She didn't finish, but he knew what she meant.

"After marrying Tate while being pregnant with my child," Dallas said.

"Yes." She forced herself to meet his gaze. "If you're waiting for an apology, you won't get one. I did what I thought was best at the time. For me, for my parents, and for Laney."

His jaw clenched, but he didn't say anything. She turned away, unwilling to discuss her decisions any further. She headed down the hall to pick out a bedroom, preferably one that was far away from Dallas.

There was no way to go back and change the past. Would she have had Laney alone if she had been able to get in touch with Dallas back then?

Yes, she would have.

But God had set out this plan for a reason. The words of another Bible verse, Jeremiah 1:5, flashed in her mind.

Before I formed you in the womb I knew you.

God had known what she'd do. God had known she and Dallas would become intimate, that she'd try to find him, then marry Tate. God had also sent Dallas back into her life now, nine years later. As a protector and the father her daughter deserved.

This was their path now. And while it concerned her to lose precious time with Laney in whatever co-custody arrangement they ultimately agreed to, she was happy for her daughter. The little girl would have a loving father guiding and caring for her from this day forward.

Maggie would just have to find a way to make it work.

———

THERE WAS nothing more Dallas wanted than to let Laney know he was her father, but first things first. He was confident they hadn't been followed, but that didn't mean they were safe.

He dug out the cameras and went to work placing them in strategic locations. This property was larger, though, than the last place, plus he didn't have quite as many cameras, so he had to make do with less coverage.

The trip wires should help. There wasn't as much foliage, so he was limited there too. But he was able to cover the few feet between the pool and the ground leading down to the lake. The path was well worn, so he couldn't place any wires there. For all he knew, there were others from around the general area who took this path.

The task took him about ninety minutes, and he was generally satisfied when he was finished. It wasn't the perfect solution, but he'd done the best he could with what he had.

Maggie was on the phone when he came inside. She waved him over. "Lieutenant? It's Maggie. I have some information that may help your investigation. Turns out, Tate sent me some legal paperwork, but tucked inside was a sheet of paper describing ghost guns and a website. The website has already been taken down, but he sent some information about ghost guns. Makes me think his murder must be related to selling them."

He listened as she went on to explain their theory that Tate had stolen those guns that were declared missing years ago and that he had gotten involved with this latest ghost gun scheme. "Technically, it's legal to buy the pieces to make your own weapon, but that also makes them virtually untraceable. No background check and no serial numbers. I really think you need to get the ATF involved. Tate could have been murdered with one of those ghost guns."

She listened for several minutes, before saying, "I'm not coming back yet, Loo. You put me on leave, remember? There is still someone out there trying to kill me. I need to protect my daughter."

It wasn't a surprise that her boss wanted her back now that she'd gotten evidence to help their case. He knew Maggie was good at her job, but he found it curious that she wasn't ready to head back to investigating.

"I'll let you know if anything changes, thanks." She disconnected from the phone. "He didn't balk at calling the ATF, so hopefully they will shed some light on the subject."

"I wouldn't mind talking to them myself." He pulled up their website on the phone and nodded. "They have a general eight-hundred number, it can't hurt to give it a try."

The call was answered by a woman who likely had the job of weeding out the nutty calls. When he explained how he was a former Navy SEAL with concerns about a possible ghost gun enterprise in the Austin, Texas, area, she put him on hold. "I'm going to transfer you to our Dallas office."

"Thanks." Less than a minute later, a guy with a Texas drawl picked up. Dallas went through his spiel again, only this time, Agent Tomlin asked several questions. "I wish I could tell you more, but this is all I know. Detective Chandler with the Fredericksburg Police Department has let her boss, Lieutenant Fernando, know this too. We're currently tucked away in a safe place to protect Detective Chandler's eight-year-old daughter."

"Can I reach you at this number if I need to?" Tomlin asked.

"Yes. And if I learn anything more, I'd like to call you back."

"I'll give you my personal cell number." Tomlin rattled off the number, and he put the phone on speaker so he could type it in. "Got it?"

"Yes, thanks." He slid his phone back into his pocket. "I'm sure your boss will hear from Agent Tomlin, he sounded very interested in what transpired here."

"Well, good." She smiled and ran her fingers through her hair. "I feel better already. I'm sure the ATF will help Fernando with the investigation."

"Yeah." The need to pull her into his arms was so great he forced himself to turn away. "I—uh, should go check on Laney."

"She's fine, look." Maggie waved a hand toward the patio doors. "Romeo is tuckered out, but she's going strong."

"That kid has a lot of energy," he muttered.

"Tell me about it." Maggie hesitated, then said, "I'm not entirely sure how to tell her about you. Without—you know —getting into the mechanics of it. She's only eight, she doesn't know anything about that."

The color blooming in her cheeks was adorable, and the urge to sweep her into his arms grew stronger. "I—uh, that's a good point. Maybe we just say that we were boyfriend and girlfriend before you got married and leave the details rather vague."

"She might ask questions." Maggie blew out a heavy sigh. "Maybe we should hold off a bit longer. It's getting more complicated by the minute."

"No, please, Mags." He reached for her hand. "Can't we just say we cared about each other, but our love didn't last because I had to serve overseas in the navy? And that I didn't know about her until now?"

"And make me the bad guy in this?" She jerked her hand from his. "She might be too young for this conversation."

He desperately wanted Laney to know he was her father. But did it have to be right now? Tonight? Still, it wasn't as if she would be old enough to understand the biology of intimacy for at least another year or so. He didn't want to wait that long.

"I'll take responsibility for not keeping in touch." He held Maggie's gaze. "When she's older, I'll also take responsibility for not protecting you the way I should have. I know I failed you, Mags."

Her blush deepened. "It takes two people to make a child," she whispered as if Laney may overhear through the glass doors. "I was just as irresponsible as you."

Tension shimmered between them as memories from the past washed over them. The very best three months of his life had taken place in the worst possible time frame.

Between deployments.

"I wish . . ." He let his voice trail off. It didn't matter what he wished. What he could have done differently.

They were here, together, now, and that was all that mattered.

"Don't say anything more." Maggie lifted a hand. "I'll try to come up with a way to tell Laney, but it may take a day or two longer. I want her to have time with you, Dallas, which is what we are doing right now. You heard her earlier, she's worried about being in danger, and with good reason. She trusts you to keep her safe."

"That's my main objective here, Maggie," he agreed.

"My job is to keep all three of you safe. But that doesn't mean she can't learn that I'm her father."

Impatience flashed in her gaze. "I'm not asking you to wait forever. Just a few days. Unless you can come up with a way to explain it without going into the gory details."

Gory details? A flash of anger hit hard, but he did his best to maintain control. "Nice to know you remember our time together differently than I do."

She threw up her hands. "What do you want from me, Dallas?"

What he wanted was for her to remember their time together as being as incredibly wonderful as he did. He wanted to know she didn't regret being intimate with him.

Maybe even that she forgave him.

In an instant, his anger evaporated. "I never meant to hurt you, Maggie."

"I know." She crossed her arms over her chest. "Those days I tried to get in touch with you were difficult. I was an emotional mess—scared, embarrassed, anxious, and happy all at the same time."

He moved closer. "If I had known, I'd have been there for you."

"Don't say that," she snapped. "You still had several years to go to meet your commitment, no way would you have gone AWOL."

No, he wouldn't have gone AWOL. And she was right, he had re-upped with the goal of being in the navy for twenty years to get his pension.

"You're right. I'm being a jerk. I'm sorry." He took another step closer. "But one thing you need to understand is that I fell for you hard. In my mind, I was planning our future together."

She stared up at him for a long moment, as if she

couldn't bring herself to believe him. His willpower crumbled, and he came closer still and gently pulled her into his arms.

"I've never forgotten you, Mags," he whispered. Then he kissed her, cradling her close. To his surprise, she kissed him back, sending his heart soaring with hope and happiness.

Deep inside, he knew in that moment he wouldn't be able to let her go.

CHAPTER TEN

Allowing herself to be swept away in Dallas's embrace wasn't difficult. She hadn't forgotten him either. She'd fallen in love with Dallas nine years ago, and those feelings hadn't entirely gone away.

But she couldn't help but shield her heart. His leaving had been devastating, especially after she'd discovered she was pregnant with his child. Maybe Dallas wasn't cut out for long-term relationships.

Laney wasn't there to interrupt them this time, so she forced herself to pull away. Her breathing was choppy, as if she'd been underwater, and she struggled to pull her thoughts together. "I—we can't do this."

"Why not?" Dallas searched her gaze. "We're both single adults who care about each other."

"Because of Laney." Maybe it was a thin excuse, but she grabbed it anyway. "The news of you being her father is going to be confusing enough, becoming involved will only add another layer of complications."

"Or make it easier," he countered.

In some respects, he was right. It would be easier to

present Laney with a ready-made family. But that was exactly why she needed to resist the urge to throw herself back into his arms. "No, Dallas. Being forced to stay together for a couple of days while running from danger isn't normal. We can't just float along on the waves of our past, we need to actively steer toward a future. Something we haven't discussed." She stared up at him. "You're renting a place in Austin. Why didn't you buy a place? Is it because you aren't ready to settle down there? Where were you living before anyway?"

"San Diego." He blew out a sigh. "Yeah, okay, I was keeping my options open. I came to have surgery and didn't know where I'd end up afterwards. But that was before I knew about Laney."

Laney, not her. She tried not to focus on the subtle difference. "Let's be honest here. We don't know each other very well. I've changed, and I'm sure you have too. We're not the same people who fell for each other nine years ago."

"I'm aware of how much we've changed, but I still care about you, Maggie."

"I care about you too." It was impossible not to after the way he'd protected them. "I realize you want to be a part of Laney's life, but don't you see? That's the reason we need to take things slow." Unlike the way they'd rushed into their relationship nine years earlier.

A whirlwind romance they'd both jumped into without considering the ramifications of his navy career. Especially his long, supersecret deployments.

"Yeah, okay. Fine. Slow." He raked his hand over his short, blond hair. "For Laney's sake."

She felt another prick of annoyance over how he was prioritizing their daughter over her. Which was the way it should be really.

Except . . . that wasn't entirely true. Yes, parents should love and provide for their children, protecting them with their lives if necessary. But when Laney was old enough to head off to college, it would be the two of them alone again. Two people with what, exactly, in common?

She had no clue.

True love had been missing from her marriage to Tate. She'd figured it out too late, that caring about someone wasn't enough.

She deserved to be loved for herself, just as Tate had deserved to be loved.

The way Dallas also deserved to be loved.

A flash of impatience hit hard. This wasn't the time or place for this. They had bigger things to worry about, like Tate's murder and the gunmen who'd tried to kill her.

She stepped back and turned to stare out at the pool. Laney had finally come out of the water. She sat beside Romeo, stroking his wet fur and talking to him. She couldn't hear her daughter's one-sided conversation through the thick glass, but she could tell Laney was full-on in love with the dog.

And based on the way Romeo gazed up at her adoringly, the feeling was mutual.

"Laney has been frightened enough over these past few days," she finally said. "Maybe staying here will help her to feel safe."

"That's the plan. I want her to feel safe too." Dallas moved away, leaving her alone. She could tell he was frustrated too, but what did he expect? That they'd just pick up their previous romance where they'd left off?

Impossible.

She headed outside, the heat hitting her like a slap in the face. "Are you finished swimming?"

"For now," Laney agreed with a grin. "Romeo is tired."

Hearing his name, the chocolate lab thumped his tail on the ground. Then he jumped up, making Laney laugh. Her daughter tossed the ball into the pool. Romeo jumped in after it. So did Laney.

"I was really thinking she'd worn herself out," her mother said wryly.

"Me too." She dropped into the chair beside her mother. "She makes me tired just watching her."

Her mother burst out laughing. "Oh my, I always said the same thing about you. Except you didn't swim like Laney. You were more obsessed with chasing butterflies, birds, anything that would fly."

"I remember." Once she wanted to be a pilot, but that wasn't practical. Being a preacher's kid meant there wasn't enough money for extravagances like flying lessons. Besides, she'd been blessed to attend college to study criminal justice. A degree that had enabled her to join the police force.

"It's really beautiful out here," her mother murmured. "The lake looks so peaceful."

She nodded. When her phone rang, she nearly jumped out of her chair. She pulled the device from her pocket with a frown. The number was from her boss, so she rose to her feet.

"Excuse me, I need to take this." She headed over to the other side of the patio as she lifted the phone to her ear. "This is Maggie."

"Maggie, what's all this about ghost guns?" Simmons demanded.

Obviously, their lieutenant had filled him in on the latest with the case. "I thought you guys would be happy to have a lead."

"Not when the ATF is planning to steamroll over us," he groused. "And it's not like we have any proof Tate's murder is related to a ghost gun scheme either. Why did you call the feds? What, you didn't think we could handle it?"

Technically, it had been Dallas who'd made the call, but she'd agreed with the strategy. "What do you know about ghost guns, Kent? I'm pretty sure involving the experts is the right thing to do. They have resources our small police department doesn't."

"They're already stomping around demanding information," he said sourly. "I hear you're the one who has it."

"I'll send you a copy of the note Tate tucked into the legal paperwork he sent me, but understand, it doesn't say much." She wondered why her boss hadn't asked for it, then shrugged. "Give me a minute and I'll send it over."

"Thanks." Kent's tone was curt before he disconnected from the call.

She went inside, found the envelope, and pulled out the sheet of paper Tate had tucked inside. Then she realized she needed to borrow Dallas's phone to take a picture.

"Dallas?" she called his name as she headed down the hallway toward the bedrooms. She heard counting and peeked around the corner to see him doing push-ups.

Dallas was three years older than she was, but pushing forty looked good on him. He was in amazing shape. But as the thought crossed her mind, he groaned and rolled over, grabbing his injured shoulder.

"Are you supposed to be doing push-ups?" She planted her hands on her hips. "Is that part of your physical therapy?"

"Not exactly." He closed his eyes for a moment, then rolled to his feet. "Did you need something?"

You. The moment the word popped into her mind, she shoved it away. "Your phone. Simmons wants a copy of the letter Tate tucked inside the legal paperwork. Apparently, the ATF got right on your tip. They've already gone to Fredericksburg."

"Sure." He handed her the device. "That was fast."

"Right?" It gave her hope that this situation would be resolved just as quickly. She took his phone, snapped the pic, and texted it to Simmons.

Her gaze went back to the legal paperwork Tate had included in the envelope. It seemed like a lot of expense for him to go through to have his lawyer draft it just to hide a note. She picked up the stack and began scanning the legal jargon.

As he'd threatened on the phone, Tate spelled out his wishes to have Laney live with him full time during the school year starting in September. As she read, she shook her head, trying to understand what he'd been thinking. As if her lawyer or any judge would agree to this.

Especially since he hadn't paid any child support in over two years.

When she reached the end of the legal mumbo jumbo, she frowned at the signature.

Mitchell Werner?

That wasn't the name of his lawyer. He had a female lawyer. She flipped back to the front page to see the name and address listed at the top of the page. Mitchell Werner, of Werner and Associates, was noted there too. Along with an address indicating the guy lived or worked in Austin.

A chill snaked down her spine. Had Tate really found a new lawyer to plead his case? Or was this another clue?

Was Mitchell Werner really a lawyer? Or something else entirely? The name didn't ring any bells, but she didn't remember Tate ever telling her the name of the guy he was working for either.

Since she still had Dallas's phone, she did a quick search on "Mitchell Werner Lawyer."

Two Mitchell Werners came up on the screen, but neither were lawyers specializing in family law, and even more telling, they didn't live in the Austin area. She tried another search, using the words "Mitchell Werner Austin Texas."

The top listing displayed a handsome guy in his midthirties. She clicked on the news article, lifting a brow when she discovered this Mitchell Werner was described as an up-and-coming entrepreneur.

A fancy way of saying a guy who invests in new business ventures.

Like selling the components for ghost guns?

Her cop instincts were screaming at her that this Mitchell Werner was the rich guy Tate claimed to be working for.

And if so, he was likely the same guy who'd hired the gunmen to kill Tate—and to come after her.

DALLAS GRITTED his teeth against the throbbing in his shoulder. Stupid move to try fifty push-ups, but he'd needed to do something physical to burn off his anger. Leaving Maggie, Laney, and Sarah alone to run ten miles wasn't an option.

"Dallas?" Maggie's hoarse voice made him frown. "I found something."

He quickly crossed to her side, peering down at the screen of his phone. "Who is Mitchell Werner?"

"I think he's the guy Tate was working for. And the one who is behind the ghost gun enterprise." She stared up at him. "I feel like an idiot, I never thought there would be another message within this legal paperwork. But Mitchell Werner isn't a lawyer specializing in family law. He's a businessman."

He whistled under his breath. "Good job, Maggie. We need to let the ATF know about this."

"It's just a theory," she said cautiously.

"At this point, they need every lead they can get." He gestured to the phone. "Call your boss back and let him know what you found. He can pass it along to the ATF guys."

She nodded and quickly thumbed through the screen to bring up the recent calls. She then put the call on speaker so he could hear too. "Fernando? It's Maggie again. Listen, I found something else in the paperwork Tate sent me. The name Mitchell Werner is listed as the lawyer who drew up the paperwork, but Werner isn't a lawyer. He's an entrepreneur. I think he might be the person in charge of the ghost gun operation."

"That's very interesting, Maggie. Hang on, I want to write this down." There was a pause, then he said, "Is that Mitchell with one L or two?"

"Two. And the last name is W-E-R-N-E-R."

"I'm sure the ATF guys are going to love this. But how did you find it again?"

"I'll send you a copy of the letterhead. I should have realized it sooner since Tate's lawyer was a woman named Janice Monroe, not a guy named Mitchell Werner."

"Hey, better late than never, right?" Fernando sounded happy. "This is a great lead, Maggie. Good job."

"Thanks." She took a quick picture of the legal letterhead and then sent it to him. "Make sure the image came through okay."

"It looks great. I'll get this to the ATF guy. Thanks again."

She stabbed the end button and handed him the phone. "I'm still kicking myself that I didn't notice the name difference sooner."

"You're the only one who could have figured this out. I would have no clue who your ex-husband's lawyer was." He lifted the paperwork. "Tate was pretty smart to use the legal stuff as a disguise."

"I guess. Although I would have preferred that he'd have picked up the phone to give an anonymous tip to the ATF directly rather than sending it to me." She rolled her eyes. "Taking the time to create this paperwork with the hidden clues and dropping it in the mail likely got him killed."

He couldn't disagree. "Maybe you should go through the information again. He may have included more than one clue."

She nodded thoughtfully, taking the stack of papers back. "I'll do that. Will you please call Laney in? She's been out in the sun long enough."

"Sure." He didn't mind going to get his daughter, although he was still irritated at how Maggie had pushed him away after their kiss and had decided against telling Laney the truth about his being her father.

He glanced over his shoulder to where Maggie had taken a seat at the table to inspect the legal documents more closely. Was postponing the conversation with Laney a stall tactic on Maggie's part?

Or was she right to hold off for a while longer?

He had no idea what eight-year-old girls knew about

sex. Just thinking about a girl Laney's age knowing any of the details made him cringe. Heaven help him, he did not want to be the one to tell her more than she needed to know.

He shook off the disturbing thoughts and headed outside. Laney was out of the pool with Romeo, the chocolate lab looking happy and tired.

"Dallas, how come you're not swimming?" Laney asked. "You said you loved the water."

"I do, maybe later, okay? Right now, we should head inside for a while."

"I need to think about something for dinner too." Sarah rose to her feet. "We may have enough ingredients to make tacos."

"But they won't be Mateo's Tacos," Laney protested.

"Hey, I like tacos, so I'm giving the idea two thumbs-up." He gestured toward the door. "Time to get changed."

Laney sighed but walked toward the doors. Her swimsuit had already started to dry in the hot sun.

Romeo padded along too. As much as he'd spent time training the lab, he sensed Laney's nonstop swimming and tossing the ball had worn the dog out. The way Romeo shadowed Laney made him smile.

He scanned the area around the property but didn't see anything amiss. Then he took a moment to flip through the camera images. All was quiet there too.

Nico had done well. This place was an excellent safe house. The lake view was an added plus. He made a mental note to call his buddy later to check in on the latest lead regarding Ava's disappearance. Not that he could help Nico find her until his current situation was resolved.

Maggie was still at the kitchen table when he headed

back inside, closing and locking the patio doors behind him. "Find anything?"

"Not yet." She didn't look over at him, her attention centered on the documents. He was impressed with her skills as an investigator. Her ex must have known she'd pick up on the issues and uncover the truth he'd hidden within.

Hopefully, there were more clues that would come to light. Spending time with Maggie, Laney, and even Sarah was amazing, but he could do without the constant threat of danger. Every one of the ops he and his SEAL team had gone on could have been their last. He'd accepted risking his life for his country, as did the other guys who served with him.

But failing to keep Mags and Laney safe was not an option.

"I wish we could get some fresh ingredients," Sarah murmured as she moved about the kitchen. "The tomatoes got squished in the cooler."

"They'll taste fine, Mom," Maggie said absently.

"I guess they'll have to do." Sarah took out the ground beef and went to work.

With their security measures in place, he relaxed his guard. He went to his room to grab his laptop, then signed into the private internet access offered by the property owner.

"What are you doing?" Maggie asked, looking up at him.

"Searching for information on Werner." He kept his voice low, hoping Sarah wasn't paying too much attention. "Why, did you find something?"

"Not yet, but there are some strange things in here that may be part of the message." She tucked a strand of her long, blond hair behind her ear, then scooted her chair closer. "See this? He mentioned child support payments of ten thousand dollars."

Guilt hit hard as he knew he owed far more than that for the eight years she'd raised Laney all by herself. "That seems reasonable."

"It's not. Tate was supposed to pay $500 per month, so this doesn't make any sense." She tapped the page. "Unless he's talking about ten grand in ghost gun sales."

He lifted a brow. "Maybe. But you would think the amount would be higher."

"Ten grand a month is plenty and could be just his piece of the pie. Or the starting point. We don't know for sure if there's more to this whole enterprise. Maybe there are illegal guns being sold along with these homemade ghost guns."

"Illegal meaning weapons where the serial numbers have already been removed?"

"Yeah. Why not?" She scowled at the papers. "It's hard to know if I'm overthinking this or if Tate had truly left more information for me to use against this guy. As it stands, I don't have squat."

"You've given us more than we anticipated, so stay focused on the positive." He turned back to his computer screen. "I'm going back to those three addresses that matched the last three digits of the license plate. Maybe I'm the one who overreacted to the black sedan getting off the interstate in a hurry. For all I know, the guy's wife was in labor or something."

Maggie burst out laughing, which in turn made him chuckle. Then her smile faded. "We shouldn't second-guess ourselves."

"You're right. As a cop, you need to absolutely trust your instincts."

They worked silently for a few minutes, each following their own leads. He liked the camaraderie he shared with Maggie and tried not to think about how great it would be for them to live together all the time.

Enough. What was wrong with him? He wasn't the type of guy to sit around daydreaming about stuff like this. He narrowed his gaze and concentrated on the task at hand.

He created a map to pinpoint the various locations that interested him. He wished he'd managed to check out all three of the addresses that matched the partial plates that Waylon had given them. Maybe there was another clue out there that he'd missed.

But they had another address to add now anyway, one belonging to Mitchell Werner. He started with that one, expecting to find a residential property in one of the upscale suburbs. Instead, the address appeared to be located in the center of the business district of the city, roughly two miles from the capital.

Did Werner have an office there? It didn't make sense that he could sell his goods from that spot without attracting attention.

He moved on from that address to the other three residential ones. By the time he had found them all, he realized one of them was much farther outside the city than the others. It was tempting to cross that one off the list, then again, that may be the key location.

"Maybe I'm losing it, but I don't see any other clues in this thing." Maggie pushed the document away. "Please tell me you have something."

"Not much, I'm afraid." He turned the screen so she could see the map he'd created too. "These are the three addresses Waylon gave us. This one"—he pointed at the one dot on the map—"had the black car with the plates that didn't match."

She stared at the screen thoughtfully for long moments. "We focused on that one because it was closest to Tate's old address." She abruptly grabbed the papers. "Wait a minute, there was another address in here. Hang on a minute."

He loved watching her work, her intense gaze scanning the documents. She muttered under her breath, then finally stabbed the page with her index finger. "Found it. I need you to put this address in too."

He did as she requested. The most recent address created a triangle. The business address was the lower left, the address where he'd seen the car with the wrong license plates was almost directly parallel, and the last address was at the top, equal distance from the others.

"I'm not sure this means anything significant." He glanced at her. "What do you think?"

She stared at the map for a full five minutes. "Zoom in on the new place. I want to see what it looks like on Google Maps."

He complied with her request, and a very nice house bloomed on the screen. Google Maps wasn't always perfect, sometimes the data was old, but the place looked pricey. Which gave him an idea.

He wasn't the most techy guy on the planet, but he knew how to look up homeowners in the Austin listing. It was how he'd vetted the owner of the house he'd rented for the past eight months. Something he should have done earlier really.

"This house is owned by a company, not a person." He felt his pulse kick up. "What was that website again?"

"We've Got Your Back dot com," she answered.

"Freedom Fighters, LLC." He nodded thoughtfully. "It

makes sense, doesn't it? We've got your back in fighting for freedom. You know how Texans love their Second Amendment rights."

She stared at him incredulously. "You really think this property here is actually owned by Mitchell Werner under this LLC?"

"Yeah, I do." He stared at the screen, wishing he could head over there right now to check the place out for himself. Instead, he knew he'd have to hand everything over to the ATF guys in charge.

Retirement was so not in his DNA. Once the danger was over, he'd really need to figure out what he was going to do for the next twenty to thirty years of his life.

Whatever that was, he hoped and prayed he'd be given the chance to do it with Maggie at his side.

CHAPTER ELEVEN

A rush of adrenaline hit hard. She and Dallas had found another lead in Tate's homicide case. They were one step closer to putting the person responsible in jail for the rest of his life.

"I'll call the ATF again," Dallas said in a low voice. "They should know about this."

It went against the grain to hand the evidence over to the feds, but it was also the right thing to do. She debated calling her boss again, then decided that would be redundant. The ATF would probably talk to him.

And if they didn't, it was because they'd taken control over the entire case.

"Hang on a minute." She put her hand on Dallas's arm. "Find out who owns these other properties. Maybe we'll find the one belonging to Tate."

He nodded and set the phone aside. "Why not? The more information we're able to give them, the better."

That had been her thought too. Maybe it was partially her ego, but she wanted to give the feds everything they would need to find this guy so she could get back to living her normal life.

Or rather, her new changed life, one that would include Dallas.

"This is interesting," Dallas said, interrupting her thoughts.

"What?" She leaned closer, breathing in his unique scent. Interesting how that scent took her back to their carefree days.

"This address, the one where I found the dark sedan, is owned by a person not a corporation or enterprise, and the man's name matches the one listed on the DMV records Waylon sent us." He turned to look at her. She was close enough to see the flecks of gold in his green eyes. "What doesn't match is the license plate. I feel certain the gunman must have swapped them. This guy is driving his car with the wrong plate and doesn't even know it."

"I agree, it's the only thing that makes sense. But what about the way he ditched you when you followed him?"

A dull flush darkened his tanned cheeks. "I must have overreacted. Maybe he was worried I had nefarious intentions. There are a lot of crazy drivers out there. Or he had some other emergency. I made us move to this place for no good reason."

"It was the right call at the time, Dallas." She gently squeezed his arm. "Neither one of us dared take a risk with Laney's life."

He grimaced, then gestured at the screen. "That's true, but I jumped into action too quickly. If I had searched first, I could have saved myself some heartache."

"Only because we know more now than we did earlier this morning. A lot has happened since then."

She could tell he was troubled by his lapse, but really,

he'd always done his best to put their safety first. "I'll do better," he muttered.

"You're doing fine. We have time now, so check on the other addresses," she urged. "And maybe you should also look at who owns the property where Tate once lived. I assumed he owned the place, but he could have been renting."

Dallas briefly covered her hand with his, then went back to work. Sometimes the site was slow to load, but he finally said, "I found it. The house where your ex lived is also owned by Freedom Fighters, LLC."

The news was enlightening while also making her feel sick to her stomach. "Tate was working with Werner while Laney was visiting," she whispered.

"It looks that way." He frowned. "It's possible the license plate was switched right there on that same street. It would explain why the addresses were located so close together."

"And it explains why the police didn't go check out Tate's house as it wasn't in his name."

"He should have had the address listed on his driver's license, though."

"Yes, but he may not have updated it." She wished she'd had the chance to search Tate's body when she'd found it. Had his wallet been left with the body? Or had the killer ditched it somewhere else? The latter was the more likely scenario. "I vaguely remember him saying he needed to renew during our divorce."

"Makes me think he didn't want to be traced back to this property," Dallas said. "Just in case anyone was able to figure out who the real owner was."

"All roads are leading back to Mitchell Werner."

"Flimsy roads," Dallas pointed out. "We don't have

anything concrete on the guy. Just your ex-husband's message."

"True." She waved a hand at the screen. "Keep searching."

The next ten minutes seemed to pass with excruciating slowness. Finally, Dallas sat back with a sigh. "The other addresses are dead ends. Well, except for the office building. No surprise that it's also owned by Freedom Fighters, LLC."

"That's three properties owned by the same company, which is a huge deal." Her gut was screaming that they were onto something. "Especially when you consider Tate had hidden much of this information in a fake legal document. Tate's been murdered, so it's possible this stuff he sent us may be enough for the feds to get a warrant."

"I hope so," Dallas agreed.

She did too. Pushing his phone toward him, she said, "Go ahead and make that call to the ATF. I could tell they were impressed with you being a former Navy SEAL."

"It's more that we both worked for Uncle Sam." He offered a wry grin. "But whatever it takes to get them to take action, right?"

"Right."

As he made the call directly to Agent Tomlin of the ATF, she leaned forward to hear both sides of the conversation. Noticing her gesture, he smiled and quickly put the call on speaker.

"Tomlin," the curt voice said by way of greeting.

"Agent Tomlin, this is Dallas Hoffman calling again. Detective Maggie Chandler and I found some interesting information."

"I'm in Fredericksburg now, are y'all somewhere close?" Tomlin asked.

"Not exactly, we're about an hour and twenty minutes away."

"Okay, maybe I'll catch up with you sometime tomorrow then. What do y'all have?" Tomlin sounded like a guy who got straight to the point.

"I told you that Tate Chandler sent his ex-wife some legal documents and that he'd sneaked a slip of paper inside describing ghost guns and a website called We've Got Your Back dot com."

"Yeah, and I need the original," Tomlin said.

"I understand. But Detective Chandler went through the entire document and found a few additional things that we believe are more clues from her ex-husband."

"Like?"

Dallas gave her a nod, so she said, "Hi Agent Tomlin, this is Detective Chandler. I hope you don't mind, we have you on speaker. I was going through the legal paperwork and noticed that the name of the lawyer my ex-husband used as supposedly drafting this co-custody agreement isn't a lawyer at all. His name is Mitchell Werner, and so far, all we can find out about him is that he's some sort of business investor."

"Okay," Tomlin said slowly. "I can see why that raised your suspicions. What else?"

She went on to explain about the addresses they'd found that were purchased under the Freedom Fighters, LLC. "This last property," she rattled off the address before continuing, "happens to be where Tate was living at one point. Unfortunately, I hadn't seen him in two years before he was killed, but the last time I dropped our daughter off, this was the address where he was staying. We discovered it also belongs to Freedom Fighters, LLC."

"That is very interesting," Tomlin said, a note of excitement underlying his tone. "Your ex hid all this in some legal paperwork?"

"He did, before he was murdered. Dallas and I both think the website Tate mentioned, We've Got Your Back dot com, is related to this Freedom Fighters, LLC. Unfortunately, we don't have any proof as the website has been taken down."

"We've got our tech team working on that right now," Tomlin said. "This is good stuff. We'll start the ball rolling on this end, but I'm going to need those original documents very soon. I'll head out to grab them first thing in the morning."

She hesitated, glancing at Dallas. Maybe she was being overly paranoid, but she didn't want to give Tomlin their address. Dallas seemed to sense her concern and gave a tiny nod in agreement.

"Agent Tomlin, I hope you don't mind, but we would like to meet you somewhere neutral." She kept her voice polite but firm. They weren't asking for permission. "We need to continue to stay off-grid until the danger is over."

"Yeah, that's fine. Like I said, we'll start working on this angle tonight rather than waiting until tomorrow. But I do need you to send me copies, though."

"Easy enough. Thanks." Dallas glanced at her. "Anything else, Maggie?"

"Not that I can think of."

"If you do come across anything else, let me know," Tomlin said.

"Roger that," Dallas agreed. "We'll be in touch tomorrow."

The agent didn't reply before disconnecting from the call. Maggie spread the documents out so that Dallas could take photos of each one, sending them via text to Agent Tomlin.

It felt good to have provided valuable information regarding Tate's murder, despite not having her badge or gun. She hadn't lost her investigative skills, although Dallas had done his share of the heavy lifting too.

"We make a pretty good team," he said in a low voice, reading her thoughts.

She couldn't deny it. "We do."

Their gazes clung for a long minute. She couldn't help wondering if this closeness would remain once the danger was over. Nine years ago, they hadn't argued over much.

But that was a brief and idyllic time without the stressors of day-to-day living and raising a child. She knew things wouldn't always be all sunshine and roses.

"What time would you like to eat dinner?" her mother asked, interrupting her thoughts.

Maggie glanced at the clock in surprise. She hadn't realized how long she and Dallas had been working. The hour was close to six o'clock. She glanced over to find Laney sitting with her headphones on, watching a show on Dallas's tablet. "Sometime soon is fine. I'm sure Laney is hungry."

"Ten minutes then," her mother said. "Clear off the table, would you?"

"Sure." She had to wait as Dallas was still taking photos of each page and texting them to Agent Tomlin. She hoped the guy would let them know what, if anything, he found on Mitchell Werner or whoever owned and operated Freedom Fighters, LLC.

By the time they had the legal paperwork tucked back in the envelope, her mother had dinner ready. Maggie crossed over to tap her daughter on the shoulder. "Time to eat."

"Just a few more minutes," Laney said, her eyes glued to the screen.

"Now, Laney. You can continue watching later."

"I'm almost finished," the little girl insisted.

She plucked the device from her daughter's hand. "You heard me." She glanced at the screen. There was a good twenty minutes left of the Disney movie she'd been watching.

"You're so mean," Laney shouted.

"Whoa, where did that come from?" Dallas asked. "You need to listen to your mother."

While she appreciated the assist, his comment wasn't necessary. "If your attitude doesn't change, you won't be swimming tomorrow."

Laney's eyes widened, and she looked like she might argue again, but then she wisely shut her mouth, crossed her arms over her chest, and shot her a mulish expression. "Fine. But I'm not hungry."

Maggie knew better, the girl had been physically active all afternoon and was likely very hungry and tired, but she held her tongue. She sent Dallas a warning glance for him to drop it too.

He frowned, nodded, and went over to help bring the taco fixings to the table. When they were seated, he glanced at Laney and asked, "Would you like to say grace?"

"No," Laney said, clearly pouting.

"Okay, I'll do it." Dallas bowed his head. "Dear Lord, we are thankful for this delicious food You have provided for us. We know there are many who are not as blessed as we are to have a nice home, a warm meal, and a swimming pool to use when we wish. Thank You for continuing to love and protect us. Amen."

Maggie hid a smile and echoed, "Amen."

"That was beautiful, Dallas," her mother said. "Wasn't it, Laney?"

"I guess." Laney shrugged as if the prayer hadn't moved her one inch. Yet it also seemed she couldn't withstand the enticing scent of tacos for long. The little girl straightened in her seat and reached across the table. "Can I have two tacos, Nanna?"

"Of course." Her mother handed her the soft shells, followed by the spicy ground beef.

Crisis averted, Maggie thought. And she was secretly glad Dallas had been given a hint of what real parenting was like.

Laney was a good kid, but she had her ups and downs like everyone else.

It was good for Dallas to see this side of child-rearing. Yet she had to admit, he was handling it well. Better than she would have given him credit for.

He'd be a great father. And maybe they should have that conversation sooner than later. The danger was likely to be over very soon.

They might have time to have a short vacation here at this beautiful home the way Dallas wanted.

A vacation that may help set the framework of their co-parenting relationship moving forward.

———

DALLAS HADN'T SPENT a lot of time around kids, other than his seventeen-year-old nephew, Jason, who was struggling with the boredom of a small town, but he was surprised at how Laney had lashed out at Maggie.

It only gave him a greater appreciation for what she must have gone through as a single parent, especially after her divorce.

The way Laney avoided his gaze told him she knew that she'd been wrong to yell at her mother. Maybe the long afternoon of swimming had caught up with her. He was no expert, but she looked tired.

"No, Laney," he warned when she tried to sneak a cherry tomato to Romeo. "I told you, no people food."

"Tomatoes are healthy," she said.

"I told you not to feed him from the table." He kept his tone even, but it wasn't easy to hide his frustration. Thankfully, Romeo was well trained. The chocolate lab sat and gazed up at Laney without taking the food.

"He looks hungry," she muttered.

"He'll eat when we're finished." Dallas swallowed a sigh. He wanted to tell her to behave but left the discipline to Maggie.

For now.

Laney pouted but ate two tacos, adding liberal amounts of hot sauce. He had to admit, she reminded him of himself at that age. His parents had passed away at the end of his first four years in the navy. His father had suffered a terrible accident, falling while working on the oil rig, while his mother had died of breast cancer. Brenda had undergone elective mastectomies when her DNA revealed she carried the same cancer gene. A brave and strong woman, his sister, especially the way her husband had left her soon after the surgery. He hoped Jason straightened himself out too.

He missed his parents and knew if they were here today, they'd adore Laney. *Even on her bad days*, he thought wryly. Looking back, he knew he'd given his parents a lot of grief, especially when he'd hit his daredevil phase.

Extreme sports like skateboarding and motocross racing and rodeo riding had been just a few of the things he'd tried. Working summers on the oil rigs with his father had given him plenty of money. He understood why his dad had kept doing the job that had eventually stolen his life. And he'd often wondered if his mom had simply given up the cancer fight after losing her husband.

His family's blood ran through Laney's veins, and for the first time, he truly understood the importance of nourishing the next generation. Long after he was gone, Laney and her children, and her children's children, would live on.

A humbling concept.

When they finished eating, he helped carry dirty dishes to the sink. Then he took a few minutes to feed Romeo, making the lab sit and wait for the hand signal before he ran over to begin chomping on his food. As a puppy, Romeo had eaten so fast he'd sometimes thrown up his food. Dallas was told to buy a doggy dish with grooves that forced the dog to slow down while eating.

Romeo was better now, he didn't inhale his food. But Dallas also made it a point to play with the dog's ears, poking and bothering him while he ate. A trick that prevented Romeo from snapping or growling at anyone who interrupted him while eating.

The way Laney was now.

"Do you like that dry stuff, Romeo? Huh?" Laney stroked the dog's head. "I bet you'd like better food than that stuff."

He sighed, wishing she'd drop the issue already. Apparently, she'd inherited some of his stubbornness. His sheer determination and grit had gotten him through BUD/S training.

At least Romeo's tail wagged cheerfully as he ate, indicating he didn't mind Laney's attention.

"I'll help with the dishes," Maggie offered.

"No thanks, dear. I'm happy to take care of them." Sarah sent him a sly look. "Don't you have something important to discuss?"

Maggie winced, and he knew that meant she wasn't ready to have the conversation with Laney about him being her father. And since the little girl was feeling a bit testy, it may not be a bad idea to wait.

Yet to his surprise, Maggie abruptly nodded. "We do, yes."

"We do?" he echoed.

She took a deep breath and nodded. Romeo had finished his food and was licking Laney's fingers as if they were a treat for dessert. "Laney? Will you come to the kitchen table, please? We need to talk to you."

Laney's gaze was full of suspicions. "Are you taking my swimming time away?"

"Not yet, but you know very well that you need to behave yourself." Maggie crossed over to sit at the table. He took the seat across from her, leaving the end seat for Laney. Now that the moment had come, he felt incredibly nervous.

Sarah was busy in the kitchen, but he knew she was listening to their conversation. He couldn't blame her. As Laney's grandmother, she had a vested interest in how they handled co-parenting Laney from this point forward too.

Laney plopped down in the chair, glancing from him to her mother. "What? I did what you asked. I stopped watching my show."

"I know you did, and I appreciate that." Maggie took a

moment to compose her thoughts. "But this isn't about the show. I wanted to tell you a little bit about Dallas."

"Dallas?" Laney's surprised gaze darted to him. "Oh, I get it. You guys are dating, right?"

He choked back a surprised laugh. The girl was smart enough to pick up on the attraction shimmering between him and Maggie, at least on his part. Based on the heat in their embrace, Mags still had feelings for him, too, whether she wanted to admit it or not.

"Not exactly, but you are right. We used to go out on lots of dates," Maggie said. "Years ago, before you were born, Dallas and I spent three months together."

Laney frowned. "You said he was an old friend."

"I should have told you he was my boyfriend back then," Maggie admitted. She licked her lips, then said, "We fell in love, Laney. And our love created you. But things didn't work out very well because Dallas was in the navy. Our time together was cut short when he was sent away on a mission. He didn't know about you, Laney. Not until recently. You remember, the day he came to see us? You were riding your bike, and that's when he found out about you."

He had to give Maggie credit for dodging the sex issue. And she'd spoken the truth because he had loved her, and their love had created Laney. He held his breath, waiting for the little girl's response.

"You mean my dad wasn't my real dad?" Laney asked in confusion.

"He was your dad because we were married," Maggie corrected. "But I loved Dallas before I married your dad."

"I know about sex, Mom. Jane's older sister told us." Laney's expression grew upset. "You had sex with Dallas, right? And you lied to me about who my dad was all this time!"

"Be careful, Laney," he spoke up, shocked at her angry response. "You need to have some respect. Your mother was all alone when she discovered she was going to have you. She tried to find me, but I was deployed on a mission on the other side of the world and unable to talk to her or help in any way. She was in a difficult situation, one that was my fault, not hers."

"But she still lied! Mothers aren't supposed to lie to their kids!" Laney jumped up off her chair, tears welling in her dark eyes. "All this time, I didn't understand why my dad didn't love me. Now I know! He wasn't my dad. You should have told me sooner. It's your fault, Mom. This is all your fault!"

"Laney, please . . ." Maggie tried to reason with the girl, but she turned and ran down the hall to her room.

The door slammed loudly behind her.

In the shocked silence, Romeo began to whine as if concerned about the yelling and not understanding what had just happened. The lab ran down the hall to Laney's door, then back to the kitchen, looking at him as if expecting him to do something.

If only he could.

"I can't believe she knows about sex," Maggie said with a groan. "Jane's older sister told them? Like what exactly did she explain? Good grief, those girls are too young to hear"—she waved a frustrated hand—"that."

Laney's knowledge of sex was the least of his concerns. This wasn't the response he'd expected. That he'd longed to have. "Honestly, Maggie, I'm more worried about her reaction to the news. I thought she'd be happy to learn the truth.

Especially since she didn't have a close relationship with your ex."

"It is my fault," Maggie said, dropping her face into her hands. "What was I thinking? I should have waited. The timing was lousy. I knew she was already grumpy, tired from the long day. This news on top of everything that has taken place was obviously too much for her to handle."

Those things were probably true.

But maybe Laney didn't want him to be her father at all.

CHAPTER TWELVE

"I'll go check on her." Maggie wrestled with guilt over dumping the truth on her young daughter's slim shoulders. As a mother, she should have handled this better.

And she was still reeling from Laney's claim she knew all about sex.

Lord, help me! Guide me!

She'd never felt so helpless.

"Give her some time, Maggie." Her mother came from the kitchen to join them at the table. "She'll come around."

"Will she?" Dallas asked, his expression grim.

"Yes." Her mother sounded firm. "She's tired, and maybe a bit confused, but she already looks up to you, Dallas. This is a minor bump in the road."

Maggie could tell Dallas didn't see it as a minor bump. And she wasn't completely sure she did either. She searched her mom's gaze. "You're sure I should give her some time alone?"

"I am, yes. She'll probably fall asleep and will feel better in the morning." Her mother patted her shoulder, then returned to the kitchen.

Dallas stared down at his hands, then lifted his gaze to her. "I don't know why I thought this would be easy."

She managed a lopsided smile. "Trust me, when it comes to kids, nothing is easy. But Laney is a good kid. I'm the one she's upset with, not you. I think my mom is right, she'll feel better after she gets some sleep."

He nodded, then slowly rose. "I'm going to walk the perimeter with Romeo."

She frowned. "You have the camera app on your phone, you know there's nothing going on outside."

He shrugged, then glanced toward the pool. "You're right. Maybe I'll take a swim instead."

"That's a good way to burn off your frustrations," she agreed. Did he have a swimming suit? She decided not to ask.

"Come, Romeo." Dallas headed into his room to change. Maggie followed, pausing to listen outside Laney's door. All was quiet inside, and she hoped that meant the little girl had fallen asleep.

She rested her hand on the doorknob, tempted to look in to check on her, then stopped and moved back. It might be better to give her daughter some time, the way her mother had suggested.

Turning, she nearly dropped her jaw when she saw Dallas walking out of his room wearing a pair of athletic shorts. Her gaze lingered on his bare back, but then she noticed the scars marring the skin around his left shoulder.

They were faded, but she knew from the way he sometimes massaged the joint with his hand that it still hurt. Foolish of him to have done those push-ups, but her heart ached for him. Dealing with physical limitations wasn't easy. She'd only been injured once on the job, sustaining a badly twisted ankle, nothing as bad as what he'd gone through.

Resisting the urge to watch him swim, she went into her room. She was exhausted, but it was too early to go to bed. Normally, she enjoyed reading in those rare moments of downtime.

But she was too keyed up to do that either.

Remembering Dallas's computer, she debated going back to continue investigating. Or maybe it was just a good excuse to watch Dallas swim without being too obvious.

She mentally rolled her eyes at her own foolishness. Thirty-five years old and she was thinking like a hormone-struck teenager.

After pacing the length of the room for a few minutes, she gave up and went back to the kitchen table. The space was empty, making her assume her mother had gone to her room, maybe to read or watch TV. Nearly every room in the house had a TV, which was a rare luxury. Through the patio doors, she noticed Dallas was swimming laps while Romeo stretched out on the concrete edge of the patio to watch. Dallas's muscles propelled him through the water with deceptive ease.

Tearing her gaze away, she went to the computer. Gawking at Dallas was wrong. There had to be something constructive she could do to keep working the case. Continuing to hang out here with nothing to do would be torture. Better to remain busy.

The map of properties Dallas had found was still up on the screen. It occurred to her that they should have called the Austin police about the swapped license plates. The guy driving the black sedan with the wrong plates should be informed about the way his real license plate was used to commit a crime.

Then again, maybe Simmons or Fernando had already taken care of it. She was so far out of the information loop she had no way of knowing what they'd accomplished. Yet she fully suspected that the ATF agents had probably pushed her boss and Simmons aside, taking over the homicides and looking to connect them with Mitchell Werner.

If that was the case, Simmons would likely tell her. She called his cell, but the call went straight to his voice mail. She frowned at the phone. Either he'd cut her off immediately because he was in the middle of something or he'd turned his phone off, which wasn't likely. Fernando liked them to be available at all times.

Whatever. Even without Tate's homicide and the gunman's death to work, there were always other crimes needing attention. Especially in her absence.

She went back to searching Mitchell Werner, trying to find him on various social media sites. But there was nothing. Which was unusual in and of itself. Granted, lots of people shied away from social media, as a cop she didn't have an account anywhere, yet a guy who invested in business should be able to be found somewhere.

The most recent article was almost three years old and happened to be the one Dallas found. It was a brief write-up in the *Austin American-Statesman* newspaper that only gave a very brief overview of the guy. The information was so vague she couldn't even say for sure how old he was.

Was this when he'd started his criminal enterprise? Tate had claimed he was working for a rich guy right after their divorce when he moved to Austin. That would have been a year earlier than when this picture had been taken.

Looking at Michell Werner, she didn't believe for one minute Tate was ever doing security work. That means they must have been in cahoots before this photo was taken.

It was unusual that a criminal would want their face splashed in the newspaper. Unless this had been taken without his knowledge. She peered closer and noticed it was a bit grainy, as if taken from a distance. Hmm. That would explain the vague details in the article.

She minimized the photo and continued her computer search. She used these types of searches in her detective role, but the criminal activity in Fredericksburg was far less serious than murder and illegal gun sales. Thankfully, most of the criminals she'd dealt with were stupid enough to leave a trail.

Not Mitchell Werner. If not for that one photograph, they wouldn't have anything on the guy.

She was confident the feds would find him, though. Pushing the computer aside, she glanced over to where Dallas was still swimming laps in the pool. Romeo was on his feet now, his head following Dallas's movements. Dallas sliced through the water so smoothly he barely made a ripple.

It bothered her that he was hurting over Laney's reaction to the news. Kids could wound their parent worse than just about anyone else, but this wasn't the way she'd expected to start things off.

She forced herself to turn away. Dallas wanted to be alone, and Romeo was out there to cheer him up. Heading back down the hall, she paused once more outside Laney's door.

Still silence from within. After another internal debate, she slowly and silently opened the door. Just a crack because she didn't want to wake Laney from sleep.

Warm air wafted toward her, which seemed odd. Wasn't the air-conditioning working in this room? She carefully pushed the door open another inch to see better.

The window leading to the side of the house was open. She swung her gaze toward the bed and froze.

It was empty.

Her heart thudded painfully against her rib cage. She pushed the door open farther, expecting to see Laney curled in a chair with a book, tablet, or handheld computer game, but the chair was also empty.

"Laney?" She went into the room and quickly searched the area. It wasn't a large room, but it had a walk-in closet, and there was also the bed. She checked both, even as alarm bells jangled in her mind.

Laney wasn't in the room. And when she crossed over to the window, she realized the screen had been moved upward. She poked her head out and called, "Laney? Come back to the house right now!"

Nothing. No response and no sign of the little girl.

Whirling from the window, she ran back through the house and out through the patio doors. "Dallas!"

He stopped swimming mid stroke, swiping water from his eyes. "What?"

"Laney's gone."

He stared at her for a long second. "Gone, where?"

"I don't know. The window in her room is open, and she isn't anywhere nearby. Hurry, we need to find her."

He vaulted out of the pool, water streaming down his sculptured torso. She barely noticed, her mind racing.

She'd had cases where parents had called to say their child had run away from home. Younger kids usually ended up at a friend's house, older kids could be more worrisome as potential victims of trafficking.

Laney had never done such a thing. Not even when she was younger and having one of those *I hate you* tantrums.

She tried to tell herself the little girl probably went to sit by the lake. Dallas grabbed a towel, dried off, and then came inside.

"I'm heading out as soon as I change my clothes. But I need something of Laney's for Romeo to track."

"Like what?"

"Clothing and her flip-flops. I noticed she wears them a lot."

She nodded and followed him down the hall. When he disappeared into his room, she went to Laney's and found a pair of yellow flip-flops and her clothes from the day before. Her damp swimming suit was also on the floor, but it smelled heavily of chlorine, so she left it.

Dallas met her in Laney's room with Romeo at his side. She could see he had the tennis ball in the pocket of his cargo pants. Dallas didn't go straight to the window but looked around first.

"I already checked under the bed and in the closet," she said impatiently. "She's not here."

"Okay, that's fine." He grimaced. "Second nature to check for myself, sorry. I've been working with Romeo on scent training, and he knows Laney well, so this should work." He knelt on the floor beside Romeo, holding Laney's flip-flops and clothing near the chocolate lab's snout. "Laney. This is Laney."

Romeo buried his nose in the clothes, then sniffed around the room, jumping up onto the unmade bed. The way he buried his nose in Laney's pillow brought a hard lump to her throat. Romeo loved Laney. She felt certain Romeo would find her.

"Laney," Dallas repeated. Then his voice grew stern. "Seek. Seek Laney!"

Romeo seemed to straighten, his sniffing growing more intense. As the lab moved toward the window, she followed.

"Hold on, Mags. I need you to stay here."

"I'm coming with you," she insisted.

"I can't let you do that. I need you here, especially if Laney returns."

"My mom is here." She sent him a pleading look. "Please, Dallas. I'll go crazy staying here."

"You can't come with me. I wouldn't make you stay back if it wasn't important." He held her gaze for a long moment. "Too many people will distract Romeo. He's not a professional K9; I don't want to confuse him."

She wanted to argue, to insist, but looking at the dog, she reminded herself that Romeo was their best chance of finding Laney. Especially if she was down at the lake. She reluctantly agreed. "Okay, fine. You better call me if you learn anything."

"I will." The words barely left his mouth when Romeo jumped through the open window. Dallas gave her a quick, sympathetic glance before he quickly followed suit.

At the window, she watched the man and dog move farther from the house, angling in the direction of the lake. The embankment was steep, but Laney was a tomboy and likely would have considered it fun to head down.

All she could do now was close her eyes and pray that God would show Dallas and Romeo the way to finding Laney.

Very soon.

DALLAS FOLLOWED as Romeo made a winding path. He didn't hesitate to give the lab room to do this thing. This job was too important to mess up, and his trainer had stressed how vital it was not to interfere while the animal was in working mode. All dogs wanted to please their handlers, so anything he did might sway Romeo away from the correct path.

It was no surprise that Romeo headed down the embankment leading to Lake Buchanan. He wasn't sure how, but the dog managed to avoid his trip wires. Maybe Dallas's scent lingered on them. As he saw the sun setting over the lake, he mentally kicked himself for not making time to take Laney down when she'd asked about it.

The reassuring part of the whole nightmare was that Laney was a good swimmer. She wouldn't drown unless something untoward happened. What if she hit her head on a rock? Slipped and twisted her ankle?

The list of possible hazards was endless, so he tried not to dwell on them.

Laney was smart and resourceful. Unfortunately, she'd also been angry and upset after hearing the news of him being her father. Which had caused her to act rashly, jumping out the window to what—spend some time alone?

He swallowed hard as Romeo headed down the path toward the lake. If Laney had stayed on the path, this should be easier. He wanted to call out her name, but he waited to see what Romeo would find.

When they reached the bottom of the path, Romeo abruptly stopped to sniff along the base of a large rock. The dog stayed there so long Dallas's pulse kicked up. Had Laney stopped there to rest? Maybe get stones out of her shoes?

No, she'd been wearing shorts, a T-shirt, and pink flip-flops when she'd been in the kitchen. She could have changed into other shoes, though, and he wished he'd asked Maggie if the little girl had brought athletic footwear along.

Romeo looked up at him and sat in front of the rock.

"Good boy," he praised without reaching for the ball. This was the tricky part of the search process. He wanted to reward the K9 for finding the scent, but the lab hadn't found his quarry yet. "Good boy, Romeo, now seek. Seek Laney."

Romeo jumped up and went back to work.

As the dog picked up the scent trail, Dallas raked his gaze over the Lake Buchanan shoreline. There wasn't any real beach-like area as a spot for visitors to use for swimming. The lake was large enough for small boats, but he didn't see a boat launch or any watercraft out on the water.

Worse, there was no sign of Laney. No people at all, which wasn't very reassuring. He'd hoped to question whoever was nearby if they'd seen her.

Romeo headed to the right, making a circle around the water. There was no path here, and he kept a keen eye out for any sign that Laney had gone this way. He trusted Romeo's nose, but he was hoping for more. Maybe Laney had brushed up against a pricker bush, leaving a thread from her clothing behind.

So far, he'd come up empty-handed. The sun was going down now, and he really wanted to find her before darkness fell.

Was she scared? Had she wandered around and gotten lost?

Romeo took an abrupt turn toward the water. There was a small, sandy area around this area of the lake. The K9 sniffed intently all along the sandy spot, then once again looked up at Dallas and sat, his ears perked forward expectantly.

"Good boy, Romeo. You're a good boy." He spoke loudly, hoping that if Laney was within earshot, she'd hear and call out to them.

But there was nothing but silence.

Romeo wagged his tail, dropping his gaze to the pocket where he knew Dallas had his tennis ball.

He didn't reach for the ball. Instead, he bent and rubbed the lab's head and ears, then knelt to examine the sandy ground. Laney didn't weigh much, but he'd hoped to see footprints she might have left behind.

The sand had been disturbed, which was odd. There was a mishmash of footprints overlapping each other. Almost as if others had come to this spot after Laney had been there.

Maybe she'd come but decided to move on when the others arrived. Although where were those same people now?

The tiny hairs on the back of his neck rose in alarm. Something wasn't right. He was sure Laney had come this way, likely stopping here to put her feet in the water to test the temperature. He could easily imagine her using the warm or cool water as a way to get him to bring her swimming down here.

"Seek, Romeo. Seek Laney."

Once again, the dog rose and went back to work sniffing the area. Twice he lifted his nose in the air to catch her scent. The trainer he'd used had taught him about scent cones and how dogs didn't just find the scent on the ground where people walked but could often capture their scent in the air, especially if they were nearby.

Nearby being a relative term since dogs could pick up scents from great distances.

Romeo turned in a circle, sniffed again, then moved away from the water. Dallas followed his K9's path while keeping a keen eye out for signs Laney had been there.

His phone vibrated. Recognizing Maggie's disposable

phone number, he quickly answered. "Did she come home?"

"No!" Alarm echoed in her voice. "I thought you would have found her by now."

"We're still following her scent trail." He did his best to remain calm. "But since you called, do you have any idea what kind of shoes she might be wearing?"

"Hang on." He heard sounds of rustling, then she returned to the call. "I don't see her pink flip-flops."

He winced, realizing Laney hadn't prepared well for the terrain. "No athletic shoes, huh?"

"She claims her toes need to breathe." There was a soft hiccuping sound, then, "Dallas, please find her. Please find my baby."

"We will. Have faith."

"I've been praying the entire time you've been gone."

"Me too. We'll find her. Romeo is working hard. I'll keep you updated, okay?"

"Okay," she whispered.

He disconnected from the call, certain Maggie had been crying. It pained him to hear her so distraught, yet he was feeling pretty unhinged himself. He forced himself to take a deep breath and listen. Maybe Laney was close enough to have overheard his part of the conversation. It was possible she was hiding out of sight, unwilling to face him.

Then again, there weren't that many places to hide. Even for an eight-year-old.

He thought about the cameras and mentally kicked himself for not checking them earlier. He quickly thumbed through them as he walked, finding the one that showed Laney wearing jean shorts and a blue-striped shirt heading down toward the lake in her pink flip-flops.

Where are you, Laney?

Romeo caught his attention. The lab was sniffing the air again, then took off up the slope, taking a route that led away from the lake.

It was strange that Laney would have chosen to go up the incline here where there wasn't any path. Especially if she was wearing flip-flops. But he wasn't about to second-guess Romeo's instincts.

Trust your dog.

The trainer's advice echoed in his mind. He shook off the uneasy feeling, knowing that Romeo might pick up on his discomfort. He trusted Romeo, and he had faith that God was guiding him.

Yet when the incline grew steep, the terrain ragged and littered with rocks, more doubts jangled in his head. Had Laney really come this way in her flip-flops? It didn't seem likely, but he kept silent, other than giving Romeo the occasional reminder to seek Laney. Thankfully, Romeo treated these searches like a game, and he was always up for having fun.

When they reached the top of the ridge, he was surprised at how far they were from the rental property. He glanced around, wondering if they were currently standing in someone's backyard. Romeo continued trotting along, sniffing and tail wagging. Then the K9 abruptly sat and turned his head toward Dallas, his long tongue lolling out of his mouth in a way that made him look satisfied with a job well done.

Dallas crested the top of the incline and double-checked to see if they were trespassing. He noticed there was a road not far away, which made that unlikely. He quickly crossed over to where Romeo sat. His heart dropped like a rock when he saw what had caught Romeo's attention.

A pink flip-flop. Not an old one but a newer-looking one. And small, as if it belonged to a child not an adult.

He knelt beside the dog, praising him even as he stared in horror at the find. He threw the ball up into the air, and Romeo leaped up to grab it, running around like a proud papa with the ball in his mouth.

Dallas tore his gaze from the flip-flop and forced himself to stand, sweeping another gaze over the area. The proximity of the abandoned footwear being so close to the road gave him a sick feeling in his stomach.

"Seek Laney." He couldn't hide the desperation in his voice. "Romeo, seek Laney!"

Romeo dropped the ball at his feet, then eagerly went to work, sniffing all along the area where he'd found the flip-flop. Dallas pocketed the ball, hoping and praying he'd pick up Laney's scent. He watched as the dog made a wide circle, sniffing all around before going right back to sit near the flip-flop.

This was it. The end of Laney's trail.

He stared helplessly down the road. He knew in his gut Laney had been kidnapped. Unfortunately, he had no idea how or where to find her.

CHAPTER THIRTEEN

Maggie moved from one window to the next, desperately searching for signs of Laney, Dallas, and Romeo around the shores of Lake Buchanan. She caught glimpses of Dallas walking near the lake, but this rental property being up on a hill made it difficult to see much of Romeo.

Her stomach churned when there was also no sign of Laney.

Please, Lord, keep my daughter safe in Your care!

The prayer didn't ease her mind. Dallas and Romeo had been outside for nearly thirty minutes. If Laney was sitting and watching the water, or had even gone swimming, they'd have found her by now.

She knew in her heart that something was wrong. Terribly wrong.

When her phone rang, she grabbed it like a lifeline. "Dallas? Did you find her?"

"I'm afraid not. Mags, I found one of her pink flip-flops near the road roughly a half mile from our rental."

One flip-flop? She stumbled toward the sofa, her knees going weak. "You're saying she's been kidnapped."

"Romeo followed her scent all around the lake and up the embankment. The trail ends here, so yeah, I think someone has taken her."

"We need to call the police. The FBI. They need to get an Amber Alert out." Her mind shimmered between cop mode and scared-to-death-mother mode.

"I'll be there soon. I can check the cameras to see if any of them caught an image of the vehicle."

"Hurry," she whispered. "I need you, Dallas. I'm so scared."

"I know. Me too." She could hear his breathing accelerate and realized he was running. Knowing she wasn't entirely alone in this gave her strength. She disconnected from the call, then crossed over to the computer. Lake Buchanan was too far outside of Austin for that police department to be notified. She had to look up who had jurisdiction over this area. Turned out to be the small town of Burnet.

As she punched in the phone number, the door burst open. Dallas and Romeo had made good time in getting back here.

"Hold on, Maggie." Dallas held up a hand. "Let's call Agent Tomlin first."

"Okay, you think he'll be a quicker connection to the feds?" Her finger hovered above the call button. "It's the locals that would issue the Amber Alert, though, right?" Holding off even a few minutes seemed impossible. What if whoever took off with Laney stopped for gas? The sooner her picture was plastered all over the media, the better.

"You're right, call the locals to get the Amber Alert started." He looked chagrined. "Meanwhile, I'll contact Tomlin. I feel certain Laney's disappearance is related to the ghost gun investigation."

She didn't disagree. The dispatcher put her through to a detective right away, who introduced himself as Detective Artes. "My daughter, Laney Chandler, is missing. She's eight years old, blond hair, brown eyes, four feet ten inches tall, and slender, weighing fifty-five pounds. She was last seen in our rental house on Lake Buchanan. One of her pink flip-flops was found about a half mile from the property near a road. I need an Amber Alert issued ASAP."

"First, we should search the area," Artes began.

"That's been done. I'm a Fredericksburg police detective, and her father is a former Navy SEAL. He and his K9, Romeo, have already searched the area, that's how they found the pink flip-flop near the road. What's your number? I'll send you a recent picture of Laney."

Detective Artes's entire attitude changed with that information. He repeated Laney's description, then rattled off his number. "I'll get this Amber Alert out ASAP, but I need to come and talk to you and her father."

"That's fine." She quickly provided the address of the rental property. "Please hurry. She's been missing for almost an hour."

"I will," Artes promised.

She lowered the phone, wishing the news of the outgoing Amber Alert made her feel better.

It didn't. If anything, she felt more helpless than ever. She needed to do something, anything to try to find Laney.

Turning, she noticed Dallas was still on the phone with Tomlin. Maybe the ATF agent could get them in touch with the FBI. She agreed with Dallas, this was more than an incidental child abduction case. Laney was smart, she wouldn't go off with a stranger.

She had to close her eyes, imagining Laney screaming

and crying out in fear as some pervert dragged her into the car.

"Thanks, Tomlin. Call me back." Dallas disconnected from the line. "He agrees that Laney's abduction is likely related to the case. He's notifying the FBI about the Amber Alert."

Again, she tried to be reassured that the authorities were involved and taking this seriously. "What else? Has Tomlin made any progress on Mitchell Werner?"

"Not as much as we'd like," he admitted.

"I'm calling my boss." Maggie punched in her lieutenant's phone number. "He needs to be aware of what's happening."

"Who is this?" Fernando asked in a cranky voice.

"It's Maggie. Laney has been kidnapped." The words tumbled from her lips. "I tried to call Simmons earlier to be filled in on what's happening with the case, but he didn't answer. I need to know what you know, Fernando. This is well beyond Tate's murder."

"Are you sure she's been kidnapped?" Fernando asked.

It was all she could do not to scream at him. "Yes, I'm sure. The Burnet police have already issued an Amber Alert. But you know Laney's disappearance can't be a coincidence. Please, tell me what you know!"

"Agent Tomlin and a female agent, Karen White, have taken over the case. We honestly didn't get very far on uncovering details about Tate's murder. No wallet or ID at the scene and no phone either, but his carrier's records indicate his last call was to you."

"But that was hours before his death," she said.

"Yes, the ME estimated his time of death to be about five o'clock in the morning. He wasn't killed where you found his body, that location was a dump site. We went to his last-known address in Austin but were told he hadn't lived there in well over six months. Some other guy is there now."

Six months? She found that interesting. "Where was he staying?"

"We're tracking his credit card, seems he's spent some time at a motel and at another rental property in Austin. So far, those places have come up clean."

It was disheartening to realize how much they hadn't uncovered. "What about the dead gunman, David Cortney? What do you know about him?"

"Not much, although I'm still mad you didn't tell us your SEAL friend was the one who shot him until after you left the scene." Reproach underscored his tone. "There were two witnesses inside the pool area who saw you, your mom, and daughter, a muscular guy with a chocolate lab, and the gunman. Their opinion indicated the shooting was self-defense, but you still should have turned yourselves in."

"I know but tell me this, Loo, if your family was in danger from a gunman, would you be so willing to stop in and chat about the recent attempt on your life? Or would you get them someplace safe? I did what I felt was necessary."

Fernando sighed. "That's the only reason you still have a job, Chandler. Because I get your concerns about your family's safety. But you know very well you and your new boyfriend aren't above the law."

To hear Dallas described as her boyfriend would have been comical under different circumstances. "You really have nothing more on this Cortney guy? What about the black sedan?"

"We didn't find a vehicle the gunman may have used at the hotel, it appears he was dropped off or had a partner that got out of Dodge when the bullets started to fly. Cortney's last-known address was also Austin, but it wasn't anywhere close to where your ex used to live."

"You need to check rental properties under the name Freedom Fighters, LLC. We think the owner of that LLC is the one behind the ghost gun scheme." She snapped her fingers. "That reminds me, we found a black sedan with a license plate that doesn't match the one listed on the DMV records. The house address was only two blocks from Tate's previous address. That guy is driving around with a stolen license plate."

"We'll look into that," Fernando said. She was glad he didn't ask how she knew about the DMV records. She didn't want to rat out Waylon, but nothing mattered other than finding Laney.

"Please, Lieutenant. You have to keep digging. Tate was involved in something criminal, and that's put Laney in danger."

"I see the Amber Alert now." As if on cue, Dallas's phone chirped with the same alert. "I'll get my beat cops out searching the area in case she ends up back here."

"Thanks." After disconnecting, she went over to where Dallas was looking down at his smartphone screen. "The alert went out?"

"Yeah." He lifted his intense gaze to meet hers. "This may be enough for the guy to drop her off somewhere, rather than risk being found with her."

It was a slim hope, but one she clung to just the same.

Her mind went back into investigation mode. If it was the gunman who'd taken Laney, how had they been found? She thought back over their actions but she couldn't come up with any way for the gunman to have located them here at Lake Buchanan.

"Maggie? What's going on?"

She turned to find her mother looking at them in concern. She winced, realizing she should have clued her mother in sooner. She hadn't mentioned Laney's disappearance right away, feeling certain Dallas and Romeo would have found her.

Now the Amber Alert had gone out, informing her mother the wrong way.

"Oh, Mom." She crossed over to put her arm around her mother's shoulders. "I'm so sorry I didn't come find you sooner. Laney took off through her bedroom window. Dallas and Romeo searched down by the lake for her but only found her pink flip-flop near the side of the road a half mile from here." Her voice began to wobble. "I—We believe Laney's been kidnapped."

"That's what the Amber Alert said, but how? Why? Who would do such a thing?" Her mother gripped her hand tightly. "Is this my fault? I shouldn't have let her stew all alone."

"It's not your fault," Maggie said sternly.

"We've put out an Amber Alert, and the feds are involved," Dallas said, his calm voice soothing and irritating at the same time. "Please know we're going to do everything possible to find her."

Maggie wanted to believe him. To believe God was watching over their precious daughter, keeping her safe from harm.

But right now her faith was thinner than smoke, swirling up and wafting far out of reach.

EVEN DURING HIS WORST OPS, Dallas had never felt this helpless. At least during an op, there was always a way to strategize their next move.

He didn't have any such strategy now.

A knock at the door snagged his attention. It surprised him until he realized it was the local police.

"Hello, I'm Detective Emilio Artes and this is my partner, Shondra Cook."

Dallas eyeballed their gold shields, then stepped back to let them in. "Dallas Hoffman, and this is Detective Maggie Chandler. Laney is our daughter. Oh, and this is Sarah Stevenson, Laney's grandmother."

It appeared Shondra was the junior member of the detective team as she primarily took notes. Dallas found himself annoyed at how Artes was using her as a secretary but told himself it didn't matter as long as they made headway on the case.

"Would you mind starting from the beginning?" Artes asked. "What brings you here to Lake Buchanan?"

Dallas glanced at Maggie, who silently nodded. They were both in agreement that the time for secrecy around their location was over. Leaving anything out could jeopardize their ability to find Laney.

"Please sit down, Detectives," Maggie said, gesturing to the kitchen table. "I'm afraid this will be a long story."

Dallas let her take the lead, after all, the entire case started with her finding her ex-husband's murdered body. He was impressed at how organized she was in relating the events that had transpired over the past few days.

He couldn't sit still, though, and found himself wandering from one side of the room to another with Romeo keeping pace at his side. The dog kept looking up at him, sensing there was something amiss. Twice the dog went over to the door as if wanting to go out to keep searching for Laney.

Dallas would go back to searching in a heartbeat if he thought there was a way to track the little girl. But Romeo had lost the scent at the flip-flop near the road. As Maggie finished explaining the events leading up to Laney's disappearing out her bedroom window, he pulled the flip-flop from his pocket and placed it on the table near Maggie.

She swallowed hard and said, "Yes, that's Laney's."

"How do you know for sure?" Artes asked.

"Because of this tiny chunk missing from the side of the sole." Maggie pointed at the indentation. "That happened the first time she wore them. She wanted me to take them back to exchange them for a new pair, but I refused."

"And this shoe caused Romeo to alert," Dallas added. "He followed Laney's scent all around the lake. The trail ended at the road."

The two detectives exchanged a knowing glance before Artes nodded. "Okay, we'll want to see the location where this shoe was found when we're finished here."

"Sure." Dallas swallowed a wave of frustration. These were all necessary steps that needed to happen, but none of it was moving fast enough for him. He turned and went back to look through the patio doors that offered a view of the lake. He imagined an upset Laney had decided to escape through the window to check out the lake. She'd made it down the embankment and then walked around for a bit.

Someone must have approached her, either when she was down at the lakeshore or making her way back up the embankment. The dropped flip-flop made him believe she fought the abductor, losing her flimsy footwear in the process.

"Dallas?" Maggie's voice made him turn from the window.

"What?"

"The detectives would like to know about how you and Romeo searched the lake." She seemed to understand his mind was miles away. "They'd like to go there too."

The area was dark now, but that wouldn't stop him. "Sure. But let's walk and talk. I'll bring Romeo so you can see how he works."

"Is he a trained police dog?" Shondra asked.

"No, but I've been doing scent training with him for months. He has a great nose and knows Laney very well as they've played together nonstop over these past few days." He glanced down at the lab and began walking toward the door. "Come, Romeo."

Romeo wagged his tail and trotted over to stand by his side. Dallas opened the front door and gestured for the detectives to join him. "Let's go."

"I'm coming too," Maggie said. "Mom, will you stay here in case Laney returns?"

"Of course." Sarah's expression was troubled. "Please find her, Detectives."

Artes and Cook both nodded solemnly, but Dallas could tell they were feeling the hopelessness of the situation too. By now, the vehicle that had taken Laney away could be anywhere. Headed for Austin, Waco, down toward San Antonio, or up toward Dallas. They could go farther west toward Lubbock or farther, like New Mexico.

A cold chill went down his spine. What if they crossed the border into Mexico? They didn't have a passport for the girl, but the border patrol was far more worried about who was coming into the country rather than heading out.

He quelled the panic rising like bile in the back of his

throat. If this was related to the ghost gun selling business, then there would be no reason to take the risk of sneaking Laney out of the country.

"Do either of you have experience with ghost guns?" Dallas eyed the two detectives.

"We know they exist, but ordering the parts and putting a gun together on your own isn't illegal," Artes said. "We don't like it, but there isn't a law against it."

"We have reason to believe these ghost guns are being specifically marketed to people who wouldn't pass a background check," Maggie said.

"That's definitely a problem," Cook agreed. "You think that's what your ex-husband was mixed up in?"

"We do," Dallas said. He stopped the group near the path and gave Romeo Laney's clothes to sniff. "Seek! Seek Laney."

Romeo lifted his snout, then lowered it, trotting eagerly down the path. He and Maggie led the way, using his phone for a flashlight. The detectives kept pace behind them. The air was slightly cooler now that the sun was down. Yet they had to step carefully to prevent tripping and falling down the slope.

Retracing his earlier path, Romeo alerted at the same spots. Each time, Dallas praised the dog but didn't give him the ball. It felt like a waste of time to go through the motions, but he forced himself to be patient.

"Romeo does seem to be following her scent," Shondra Cook said thoughtfully. "I'm impressed."

He glanced back and nodded. "Romeo has a keen nose. He's very good."

It pained him to walk the entire path Romeo had taken earlier, but it seemed the lab was impatient too. He sniffed, alerted, then barely waited for his reward before taking off again.

Ten minutes later, they made their way up the rocky embankment to where Romeo had found the flip-flop. This time, the dog sniffed all around the area, as if upset the pink shoe wasn't there, before finally sitting down to look up at him expectantly.

Even though this exercise had been for the benefit of the detectives, he threw the ball up for Romeo to catch. The dog leaped into the air, catching the ball before it hit the ground, then ran around with it in his mouth.

"The flip-flop was here, and as you can see, the road is only ten feet away." Dallas walked the short distance. "I asked Romeo to keep searching for the scent, but he ended up right back here. Based on the flip-flop, I'm certain this is the end of the trail."

"Did you check the cameras?" Maggie asked.

"Yeah. There's nothing. Not a car in sight." He wished he'd gotten longer range cameras, but his intent was to have a wide lens to keep the perimeter of the property within view.

Not to visualize a portion of the road located a half a mile away.

"Cameras?" the detectives asked. "Do they show Laney leaving?"

"They do." He flipped through the phone images to show them. "You can see her here, wearing shorts, a blue-striped shirt, and pink flip-flops, heading down toward the lake."

Maggie crowded close, staring wordlessly at the screen. He knew what she was thinking, the same idea had crossed his own mind.

Was this the last image they'd have of Laney looking alive and unharmed?

He wasn't a pessimist by nature. He wouldn't have survived BUD/S training or being a member of the SEAL team for twenty years if he hadn't counted on sheer determination, faith, and strength to get him through the dangerous situations they'd faced every day.

But it wasn't easy to find that same positive attitude now. He swept his gaze over the rural area.

Lord, hear our prayer! Keep our daughter safe in Your care!

"Where's the closest gas station?" Maggie asked. "Or any retail place that might have cameras?"

"There's a gas station five miles from here," Artes said. "We'll check it now."

Dallas took the same shortcut through the neighbor's yard to get back to the rental property. The detectives climbed into their vehicle, promising to keep them up to date with anything they found.

Dallas stood outside for a moment, looking down at Maggie. "I failed to find her," he whispered.

"You and Romeo did what you could." Tears shimmered in her eyes. "I'm so scared, Dallas. What if they hurt her?"

"I know it's hard not to imagine the worst. But if they took her because of the case, they're not going to do anything drastic."

"Kidnapping is drastic," she said harshly.

"Yes. But why? Why risk taking an eight-year-old kid? Laney wouldn't go without a fight. And she's big enough that it probably wasn't an easy task to get her into the car against her will."

Maggie blinked. "You think they want her as leverage to use against me."

"Yeah. It's the only thing that makes sense." He didn't like it, but it was slightly easier to deal with than a child-trafficking scenario. "I'm surprised they haven't contacted us with some sort of demand."

"Me in exchange for Laney?" Maggie brightened. "Of course! That would make sense. I'll gladly exchange myself for her safety."

"Whoa, you're not doing any such thing." He scowled, hating the idea of losing her or their daughter. "That's a nonstarter. Instead, we'll work toward setting a trap to get Laney back."

"Use me as bait, then, I don't care." Her dark gaze was defiant now. "Getting our daughter back is our primary mission."

He admired her willingness to sacrifice herself, he had done that and more for his country. But he wasn't losing Mags or Laney.

"Let's go back inside." He reached for the door, then stopped when his phone vibrated. He grabbed the device, swallowing hard when the call was from an unknown number. He briefly showed Maggie, then put the device on speaker. "This is Dallas Hoffman."

"We have your daughter." The voice was mechanically distorted, sounding like a caricature of a bad TV show. "If you want her back unharmed, you need to call off the police."

He froze. How had the kidnappers known? The Amber Alert? Maybe. But he turned to sweep his gaze over the area anyway, wondering if they were being watched.

"The cops are gone," he said bluntly. "I'll keep them out

of it, but only if you let me know Laney isn't hurt. I want to talk to her."

He held Maggie's gaze as they waited. Then they heard her voice. "Dallas? Mom? Are you there?"

"We're here, Laney," Dallas said. "Be brave, we're going to get you out of there."

"Da—" Laney's voice was cut off mid word.

"Laney!" he shouted.

"Enough," the mechanical voice said. "Cancel the Amber Alert and we will talk again. If you don't . . ."

The line went dead. He instantly tried to call the unknown number back, but the call didn't go through.

Call off the Amber Alert? The request hadn't been what he'd expected and made him think they weren't too far away or they wouldn't care so much.

He sensed this was just the beginning of the dance they'd be forced to perform with Laney's kidnappers.

A stall tactic? Maybe.

But what haunted him the most? The end game.

Once the kidnappers had what they wanted, there was no reason to keep Laney, or any of them, alive.

CHAPTER FOURTEEN

Calling off the Amber Alert was the last thing Maggie wanted to do. They desperately needed some savvy citizen to notice Laney looking frightened and to call the police. Yet what if the kidnappers hurt Laney? She'd do whatever was necessary to keep her daughter from being terrorized any further.

Was it even possible to call an alert off? If she claimed Laney had returned, wouldn't the detectives want to come and talk to the little girl about her abduction?

Of course, they would.

For the second time in her life, the first being when she discovered she was pregnant with Dallas's child, she didn't know what to do. She didn't want to make a mistake, like she had nine years ago. If she hadn't married Tate, they wouldn't even be in this situation.

"Dallas." She gripped his arm tightly. "What should we do?"

"Let's get inside." He held the front door open for her, then followed her in. Romeo padded into the kitchen and stretched out on the floor, looking up at them. The dog sensed their tension, but there wasn't anything she could do to fix that.

Never in her worst nightmares had she expected Laney to be kidnapped.

"Did you find anything?" her mother asked.

"No." Maggie couldn't find a way to reassure her mother either. There was a crushing weight on her chest that wouldn't ease until they had Laney back.

"I'm calling Tomlin again," Dallas said. "We need to talk this through with the FBI."

"Wait, please hold off. The kidnappers—" She abruptly stopped, realizing her mother didn't know about the mechanical voice contacting them from an unknown number. "Just give me a few minutes."

"A few minutes could mean Laney being hurt or worse," her mother protested.

Her mother was right, and so was Dallas. She knew better than to simply give in to the kidnapper's demands. There was a reason the United States didn't negotiate with terrorists. There was no trusting that the person on the other end of the call would really hold up their end of the deal.

Ninety percent of the time, they didn't.

Yet doing the right thing, keeping the authorities involved, was so much more difficult than she ever imagined. Logic meant nothing when your child was in grave danger.

Nothing.

Dallas moved away to make his call. She sank into the closest chair and covered her face in her hands. They needed a clue, something to go on. There had to be a way to find Laney.

Please, Lord, please keep Laney safe. Grant me the

strength to find her, please?

What did the kidnappers really want?

She lifted her head and looked over at the original documents that Tate had sent her. She'd already turned copies over to Agent Tomlin, but maybe the kidnapper didn't know that. She pulled them closer, wondering if there was something she'd missed. Yet if obtaining the documents was the ultimate goal, why tell them to call off the Amber Alert? Wouldn't they just arrange a simple exchange? The longer they held off on making their arrangements, the longer she and Dallas had to come up with a way to capture them.

There had to be more going on. What? She had no clue.

She read through the legal document Tate sent for what seemed like the umpteenth time, taking a moment to look at each sentence alone and in conjunction with the next one. She thought she'd uncovered all the secrets Tate had hidden within, but maybe not. She was desperate to do something constructive.

"The feds will be here in an hour," Dallas told her.

"Thank the Lord," her mother whispered.

Maggie could only nod, her emotions rolling all over the place. What could the feds do that they couldn't? Provide backup, but that wasn't going to find Laney.

They needed to figure out where she was being held.

"Maybe we should check the motels in the area." She glanced at Dallas. "We might find the black sedan."

"I'm sure the Burnet police will do that," he told her. "We gave them every bit of intel we had."

"I know, but . . ." She shook her head helplessly.

"They have every cop on their force looking for her," Dallas said gently. "Have faith in their ability."

Easier said than done. She gave a terse nod and forced herself to turn back to the documents. Concentrating on every word and sentence was extremely difficult as her thoughts kept going back to Laney.

"How did they know she was down at the lake?" She sat back and looked up at Dallas. "Taking her must have been a crime of opportunity."

"I know, that's been bothering me too. Especially since we should have been safe here. No one knew we were renting this place."

She shivered, despite the warmth. "Maybe they're tracking your phone."

"Maybe, if they got my license plate number, they may have been able to track down my cell phone carrier." He grimaced. "Either way, I can't get rid of it now."

That was true, the phone was the only link they had with the kidnappers. She wished Dallas had gotten a disposable phone for himself.

"Do you trust your friend?" She searched her memory. "Nico?"

"With my life." Dallas spoke without hesitation. "Nico would never betray me. Or you and Laney either. He's not the leak, Maggie. I promise."

She honestly didn't suspect him, but she had to ask. She rose and paced. "Then how did they find your number?"

"They have Dallas's phone number?" her mother asked.

"Yes." She gave up trying to protect her mother. "They called, and we were able to speak to Laney very briefly. They told us to get rid of the Amber Alert, but I don't even see how that's possible, considering the detectives would want to talk to Laney if we suddenly claim she's been found."

"They must be nearby," Dallas said. "I'm not going to wait for the feds. It's time I head out to search. I'm taking Romeo too. Maybe he'll find a trace of Laney's scent."

"Please let me come with you," she begged.

"You need to be here when the feds arrive. Besides, I need to move swiftly and silently. You'll only slow me down."

It wasn't easy, but she nodded in agreement. "Let me know if you find something."

"I promise." He turned and headed for the side door leading to the garage. "Come, Romeo."

The lab eagerly trotted over to join his owner. She watched Dallas slip into the garage, knowing he'd take the side door from there.

Was he wrong about the kidnappers being close by? She knew they must have been close enough to see Laney escaping through her bedroom window, but that didn't mean they kept her close to the property.

Yet how far away would they be if they wanted to make an exchange? Sure, they could pick another location, but it would have to be somewhere remote with plenty of open space around them to avoid being caught.

Which brought her right back to the Lake Buchanan area.

The minutes dragged by slowly. She continued reading through the documents, but she kept having to go back to the beginning as her mind wandered.

Her mother busied herself in the kitchen, seeking refuge in baking. She was making chocolate chip cookies, Laney's favorite. It seemed they were Dallas's favorite, too, because he'd picked up some premade chocolate chip cookie dough. Her mom usually made them from scratch, but this would suffice.

She prayed her daughter would be there soon to enjoy them.

Fifteen minutes after Dallas and Romeo had left, her phone vibrated. She startled badly, fumbling for the phone.

Then frowned when she noticed it wasn't his number but Simmons. "Hey, Kent, what's going on?"

"I have something you need to see." He spoke in an urgent tone as if he was excited. "Can you meet me?"

"Um, maybe." She glanced over her shoulder at her mother. As long as someone was here to talk to the feds, she could maybe leave for a short period of time. "But what is it that you found?"

"I don't want to talk about it over the phone. I'm about twenty minutes outside of Austin, where are you? Where can we meet?"

"I'm not far from there." She thought about the gas station that the detectives had mentioned earlier. "Hang on." Using Dallas's computer, she found the gas station and the small motel nearby.

"Hey, I just passed a sign for the White Horse Inn. Would that work?" Simmons asked.

She nodded, it was the motel closest to the gas station. "Yes, that's good."

"Great, I'll meet you there. Oh, and bring those documents your ex-husband sent to you. I think what I have helps clarify some of the information you found."

Her pulse spiked at the thought of finding something that would help Laney. "I can be there in ten minutes." Probably quicker, but that was okay. She could check the place out while she was there.

"Looks about the same time for me," Kent agreed. "Thanks for doing this. I have a feeling we're going to break this case wide open."

"I hope so." She figured he'd seen the Amber Alert, so she didn't bother mentioning it. "Ten minutes," she repeated before ending the call. She turned and grabbed the keys to the SUV that Dallas had left on the table. Thankfully, he hadn't kept them in his pocket. She glanced at her mother. "I have to run a quick errand. I'll be back shortly."

"Wait, what about the FBI?"

"They're still at least thirty minutes out. I'm sure I'll be back before they arrive. But if not, give them some cookies and ask them to wait."

"But, Maggie . . ."

"Gotta go," she interrupted. Without giving her mother a chance to continue arguing, she hurried out to the garage and slid behind the wheel of the SUV. When she opened the garage door, it sounded incredibly loud in the silence, and she wondered if Dallas was close enough to see or hear her leaving. If so, he wouldn't be happy.

Too bad. Making him angry wasn't enough to prevent her from going. Maybe Simmons had found something critical that would point them straight to where Laney was being held. Or by whom.

It wasn't until she was on the road that she realized she'd left Tate's documents behind. She hesitated for a moment, then kept driving.

She wasn't going back now. She'd bring whatever Simmons had to show her back to the rental property if needed. Besides, she wasn't entirely sure how anything Simmons had would fit with the legal paperwork Tate had sent her.

Unless it was some sort of code? He had hidden evidence within the documents, had she missed something?

Gripping the steering while tightly, she drove away from Lake Buchanan toward the White Horse Inn. The silence closed around her, so she prayed out loud. "Lord, I know I haven't been worthy of Your grace, but I'm begging You to help me find Laney, please?"

And for the first time since finding Laney's empty bedroom, she felt a sense of calm wash over her.

She was reassured by the sensation, feeling confident that God was guiding her now.

DALLAS HAD GONE to the closest neighbor first. The place was dark, and while he took the chocolate lab all around the house and property, Romeo didn't alert on Laney's scent.

He quickly moved on, heading toward the next closest neighbor. He hoped and prayed he wasn't just spinning his wheels out here, but what else could he do?

Sitting around doing nothing was impossible, and he had to squelch a flash of guilt over leaving Maggie behind.

The next house had a light on in the living room. Dallas sneaked up to peek inside. An older man with short, gray hair was watching television, some news channel. The guy didn't look like a kidnapper, but he wasn't taking any chances. He gave Romeo Laney's scent and softly told him to seek.

The K9 obediently dropped his head and sniffed along the house, going toward the door, then around the other side without alerting. Moving stealthily, he took Romeo around the entire property but still came up empty.

Swallowing a lump of dejection, he quickly moved on. He lightly jogged down the road to the area where the flip-flop had been found. He decided to take the road farther east, toward Burnet.

There was a curve in the road, and when he saw the

glow of headlights approaching, he dropped near some scrub brush, flattening himself against the ground. "Down, Romeo," he urged. The lab obediently stretched out next to him. Thankfully, the lab's dark coat worked in their favor.

Only the most astute driver would see them, and only if he or she was actively searching for a man and his dog.

After another few minutes, the SUV came into view. He didn't move but tracked the vehicle through the brush. Then frowned when he caught a glimpse of a blond-headed woman behind the wheel.

Maggie? Where was she going? He jumped to his feet and pulled out his phone. She answered on the second ring.

"Dallas? Did you find something?"

"Yeah, you driving my SUV past me, heading toward Burnet. What's going on?"

"Simmons called, claims he found something to show me related to the case." She didn't sound the least bit apologetic. "Don't worry, I won't be gone long. The feds haven't shown up yet. And my mom is there if they do. You haven't heard from the kidnappers yet, have you?"

"No." He didn't like the way she'd taken off without telling him. And what had Simmons found anyway? "Come back and pick me up. Romeo and I will go with you."

"No, I promised to meet him at the White Horse Inn in ten minutes. Besides, it's more important for you and Romeo to keep looking for Laney. I'm not sure whatever Simmons has to show me will really help anyway. Please, Dallas. Keep searching for Laney. I don't think this meeting will take long."

He didn't like it. Not that she wasn't a capable detective, but he still didn't like it. Was he being overprotective? Maybe.

"Fine, but you better call me when you're heading

back." He knew he sounded cranky. "I don't like you heading off on your own."

"You did," she shot back. "I'll keep in touch. Maybe I can pick you up on my way back to the rental property."

"Okay, fine." He pocketed the phone, still not happy. He swept his gaze over the area, trying to decide which way to go, then he knew it didn't matter. There was only one place he could go. He glanced down at Romeo. "Ready to run, boy?"

The lab wagged his tail.

"Let's do it." Running was the one activity that didn't bother his shoulder too much. Swinging his arms didn't cause the same level of discomfort as raising his arm over his head or lifting weights.

Maggie had a big head start, not to mention a vehicle that would easily outdistance him. Yet as silly as it sounded, he couldn't ignore the itch along the back of his neck. He had to get to Burnet. He picked up his pace and took a shortcut to save some time. The terrain was rocky and difficult to navigate in the dark, but he'd been in far worse situations.

Central Texas was a piece of cake compared to Afghanistan.

When he passed a house that appeared deserted, he made a quick detour toward it. There were no lights anywhere, but that didn't mean anything. For all he knew, there was no electricity running. Still, it was off the beaten track and looked neglected.

"Seek Laney," he whispered to Romeo.

The dog went into search mode. He sniffed along the ground, then broke into a trot. Dallas followed. Taking time to clear the place would put him further behind, but he didn't dare ignore it.

Not when it was the perfect place to hold a kidnapped child.

Once he got inside the place, it was easy to see no one had been there recently. The dust on the floor hadn't been disturbed. Through the multiple holes in the roof, he could see dozens of stars dotting the sky. There was mouse dirt everywhere, along with other armadillo prints. The walls were half rotted, and he suspected a strong Texas wind would flatten the place sooner or later. And the last most important thing was that Romeo hadn't alerted.

It was a bust and a complete waste of time. He tried to shake off the frustration as it had been necessary to check it out. He knelt beside Romeo for a moment, checking his paws. He'd given the K9 water before they'd left, but he wished he had more to give the animal now.

"Come, Romeo."

After heading outside, he broke into a run, determined to catch up with Maggie. Or at least meet up with her in Burnet. He kept a keen eye on Romeo to make sure the K9 was doing okay.

As much as he wanted to be a backup for Maggie, he wouldn't risk harming his dog. Romeo had run with him plenty of times, but not usually in the dark over rough terrain. He reminded himself he could always drape Romeo across his shoulders and carry him.

It would strain his shoulder, but that didn't matter. Something bothered him about the way Maggie had jumped at the chance to meet up with her fellow detective.

Not jealousy, although he hated to admit he'd felt the green-eyed monster eating at him when she'd married Tate. But that was nine years ago. No, he knew Maggie's relationship with her coworkers was strictly professional.

His uneasiness was difficult to articulate, so he didn't

bother to try. He'd spent the past twenty years of his life listening to his gut, and he wasn't about to second-guess it now.

In the distance, a gas station light illuminated the sky. Remembering Detective Artes's comment, he figured this was the station located five miles from where they had been, and it probably had security cameras.

But Maggie wasn't meeting Simmons at the gas station. She'd chosen the White Horse Inn.

Or had Simmons chosen it?

Sweat dampened his shirt, rolling down his temples. Yet an icy finger of fear trailed down his spine.

"You okay, boy?" he asked.

Romeo's tail wagged as if in agreement. The dog was panting, his tongue lolling to the side, but he wasn't concerned. Dogs didn't sweat like humans, they panted. He didn't think the canine was being overtaxed. At least, not yet.

It didn't take long to reach the gas station, the lights seemed unbearably bright after being in the darkness for so long. Shielding his eyes with his hand, he looked at the two vehicles sitting at the pumps.

Neither was a black sedan or his SUV.

He swung around the back of the building, then caught sight of another sign. A red neon vacancy sign. It was less than a mile up the road and appeared to be across the street from a family-style restaurant.

The White Horse Inn? A fancy name for what was basically a small motel that in all likelihood rented rooms by the hour.

He prayed Detectives Artes and Cook had already vetted the place. Frankly, that type of motel should have been at the top of their list. Maybe he should have listened to Maggie's suggestion to check out the motels for themselves. Well, there was no time like the present to do just that.

"Come, Romeo," he said, breaking into a run again. It only took five minutes for him to get close enough to see the structure more clearly.

He noticed several cars in the parking lot, but he couldn't see anyone sitting inside them. He frowned. Had Simmons gotten a room?

He took a moment to catch his breath from his long run, then moved forward as silently as possible. With Romeo's panting beside him, they weren't nearly as quiet as he'd have liked. But so far there wasn't anyone outside to hear them.

Less than a minute later, he found his SUV. Placing his hand on the hood, he found the engine was still warm. Maggie may have driven around a bit before pulling up to park.

The vehicle to the right of his SUV was a black pickup truck. It was well kept and had the usual gun rack mounted in the back. Minus the rifle.

Trucks were very common in Texas, and it wasn't the sedan the gunman had used, but he crept closer anyway to feel the hood.

It was cool to the touch. Because Simmons had gotten there first? Maybe. He did a quick check of the other two vehicles, one was a Jeep and the other a rusty beige sedan. Both of those vehicle engines were also cool.

Not helpful, but again, they needed to be checked. Romeo was panting less now, which was good. The room directly across from his SUV had a light on, so he sidled up and peered through the gap in the shades.

At first, he didn't see anything. He tried to adjust his

angle without giving himself away when a tall figure suddenly moved in front of the window.

Simmons? He had never met the guy, so he couldn't say for sure. He waited until the figure moved out of the way.

That's when he saw the gun in his hand.

The alarm bells went off full force. Maggie had walked into a trap. Was the guy inside the room really Simmons? Or someone pretending to be the detective?

There was no way to know for sure.

Either way, she'd been deliberately lured here. He wanted to bust in through the door but forced himself to stay where he was. He needed to get eyes on Maggie.

The man with the gun walked back and forth in front of the window two more times before finally moving far enough away to give him a bird's-eye view of the small room. Maggie was sitting on the bed, her back up against the headboard and her hands folded together and resting in her lap.

It gave him pause. Maybe they were just talking. Maybe this wasn't a hostage-type situation. He hesitated, then decided to listen to his gut. And his instincts were screaming at him that Maggie was being held against her will.

He watched for another minute, then slowly backed away from the room, giving Romeo the hand signal for come. The dog silently went with him.

He took one deep breath, letting it out slowly. Okay then.

Time to devise a plan to get Maggie out of there.

CHAPTER FIFTEEN

"I can't believe you didn't bring the paperwork!" Kent Simmons's voice rose, revealing a hint of panic.

Simmons was involved in the ghost gun scheme. Maggie mentally kicked herself for not considering him a suspect sooner. The guns that were allegedly stolen four years ago must have been taken by Kent not Tate. And Tate had the ability to track down Dallas's cell phone too.

It was difficult to fathom that the man she'd looked up to as a mentor was nothing more than a crooked cop.

"Fearing for my daughter's safety was distracting," she said calmly. "If you would have just left her alone, none of this would have happened."

"You should have brought the documents! I needed you to cooperate!" Kent was clearly not listening to reason. His agitation grew worse, and she feared he was becoming unhinged.

More so than he was already. Only a desperate man would have kidnapped an eight-year-old girl.

"Where is my daughter?" She stared at him, her muscles tensed as she mentally prepared for him to aim and shoot. "We'll exchange the documents for Laney. That was your intent all along, wasn't it? I'm sure Laney went with you willingly at first, knowing you were my fellow detective. But then you scared her, didn't you? That's why she dropped her pink flip-flop. Which we found by the way."

"Stop!" Simmons shouted. "I need to think. There has to be a way to salvage the situation. I can't blow it. This was my last chance!"

She didn't quite understand what he was talking about. Obviously, he feared the documents Tate had sent her implicated him in some way. If so, it had been cleverly hidden so that she hadn't found it. Regardless, didn't he realize the ATF already had a copy?

He may not know that; besides, a copy wouldn't stand up in court. Only the originals would. Maybe that was the truth behind all of this.

"Are you working for Mitchell Werner too? The way Tate was?" She felt the best way to get control over the situation was to keep him talking.

He flinched as if she'd punched him, but then he glared at her. "You don't know anything about it."

"I know Tate was murdered. Likely by one of the gunmen sent by Werner." She subtly shifted closer to the edge of the mattress. He'd forced her to give up her gun, but her plan was to rush him when he least expected it. Deep down, she'd hoped he'd hesitate before shooting her. They had worked closely together for the past four years, for the same police force for eleven. He couldn't be completely indifferent toward her.

She hoped.

"Kent, you need to listen to me. There's still time for you to change the course here." Another subtle shift forward. "The path you're on now? You're driving straight into tornado-force winds. Tate was brutally murdered, do you really want to be next?"

He flinched again as if imagining being shot like Tate. "Here's what we're going to do. We'll get back into your SUV and get the documents. Once I have them, I'll let you know where Laney is."

She didn't believe him, he was too distraught for this to end so easily. No, she felt certain he'd kill her the moment she gave him what he wanted.

The only reassuring part about discovering Simmons had kidnapped Laney was that she felt certain he hadn't hurt the girl. Yet she also couldn't figure out where he was keeping her. Not back in Fredericksburg, but maybe somewhere in Austin? Simmons had taken a lot of personal days over the past few months, maybe because things were heating up in the ghost gun business.

She wanted to kick herself again for not suspecting him sooner.

"That's fine. We can go back to the house," she said calmly. She prayed the FBI wouldn't show up until after they'd gotten there. Finding a strange vehicle in the driveway might send Kent off the deep edge. "But you need to tell me where Laney is. Please, Kent. You don't want to be responsible for hurting a little girl, do you?"

He didn't answer, and in that moment, she realized his plan didn't include letting Laney go. How could he? Her daughter knew him and would tell the authorities about him.

The knowledge steeled her resolve. Going back to the house wasn't an option.

She needed to find a way to take him down here.

The moment Kent used his gun to wave at the door, indicating they were leaving, she sprang from the edge of the bed, launching herself toward him. At the exact same second, the motel room window shattered; a loud thumping noise indicated something heavy had landed on the floor. She ignored it, hurtling herself against Kent. Her momentum carried them back against the door.

She grabbed his wrist, trying to wrench the weapon away, but he was bigger and stronger. He rammed his elbow into her gut, nearly making her puke, but she didn't let go.

A dog barked loudly, and suddenly Dallas was standing there, his gun pressed against Kent's temple.

"Let her go or die," Dallas said harshly.

Simmons froze. She wrenched the gun away. Then she scrambled to her feet, putting a hand on Dallas's arm. "Wait, don't shoot. He knows where Laney is."

"Go ahead and kill me," Kent said grimly. "You'll save him the trouble."

"Who? Werner?" She stepped closer despite Dallas's narrow glare warning her to stay back. Dallas was on his right, so she took a position near his left side. "Give us something, Kent. Cooperate with us and we'll convince the feds to go easy on you."

"A cop in jail will never have an easy time," he said wearily. His previous agitation was gone now, replaced with a grim acceptance. "Shoot me. I'd rather it be quick and painless."

"You want quick and painless? Then tell us where Laney is." Dallas pressed the gun more firmly against his temple. "If you don't talk, I'll shoot you in the kneecap. I hear that's excruciating."

Maggie swallowed hard, knowing Dallas wasn't bluffing. "Tell me where Laney is. She's innocent, none of this is her fault."

A crack of gunfire came from somewhere outside the

motel. Maggie instinctively threw herself to the side seconds before feeling the whiz of a bullet pass by, embedding in the drywall across from the doorway. She stared in horror at the large, red stain spreading across the center of Kent's shirt. She looked frantically from his bloody chest to the hole in the drywall as realization dawned.

Someone had shot him through the door!

Her former mentor held her gaze for a moment, then his eyes went unfocused.

"No!" She stumbled forward toward Kent as if she could prevent the inevitable. "You can't die! We need to know where Laney is!"

She belatedly realized Dallas wasn't there. Movement from the corner of her eye drew her gaze as he vaulted through the broken window and took off after the mysterious gunman. Romeo followed, hot on his heels. There was a steel garbage can sitting on the floor. Dallas must have used it to break the window.

She let them go. The gunman wasn't important. Her attention remained focused on her fellow detective. "Kent, please." She shook his shoulders. "Stay with me! Come on, I need you. Tell me where Laney is!"

His head lolled to the side, his entire body limp.

It was too late. Kent was dead.

She hung her head in despair, having no idea where to find her daughter.

DALLAS SPRINTED after the dark sedan, aware of Romeo keeping pace at his side. He aimed his Sig Sauer at the rear of the car and fired repeatedly at the vehicle. He didn't stop until the car swerved off the road, his bullets striking the rear tires and the gas tank, rendering the car inoperable.

Keeping his gun up, he continued running toward the now stalled car. No way was he letting them get away.

As if on cue, a figure emerged from the passenger-side seat of the car and ran.

"Get him," Dallas ordered. Romeo took off like a shot, seemingly enjoying the chase. He wanted to join his K9 but needed to check on the driver.

Unless the guy running away was the driver? He hadn't been able to tell if there were two people in the car or one.

He pushed himself harder, reaching the car within seconds. Finding no one inside, he spun and took off after the figure retreating in the darkness.

His previous running to reach Maggie had sapped some of his strength, but thankfully, a renewed surge of adrenaline hit hard. He double-timed it, desperate to get to the guy as quickly as possible.

As the driver slowed his pace, Romeo lunged and clamped his mouth around the guy's ankle. He screamed and hit the ground, then slowly turned his gun toward Romeo.

"Don't even think about it," Dallas shouted, raising his weapon. The guy looked surprised to see him, and in that moment, Romeo let go of his ankle and leaped up onto his chest, barking ferociously in his face.

"Get him off me!" The man shoved Romeo, and the dog slid off him. Dallas knew the dog would try again, but the brief distraction was all he'd needed.

Dallas threw himself on top of the guy, pinning him to the ground. The guy groaned, then screamed as Romeo clamped his teeth around his gun hand.

"You're finished," Dallas said breathlessly. He quickly

disarmed the guy, praised Romeo, then hauled him to his feet. "Where's the girl!"

"What girl?" The gunman appeared confused.

"The girl you kidnapped!"

"I don't know anything about a kidnapping!" The guy's voice rose in panic. As if he was more afraid of being arrested for kidnapping than murder. "I was only to take care of one situation, I had nothing to do with a kidnapping."

Unfortunately, the perp's reaction came across as all too real. His heart sank. Had Simmons been the only one involved in Laney's kidnapping? Police sirens wailed, flashing red lights drawing closer.

Grabbing the discarded gun by the barrel, still hot from the recent shooting, he smoothed a hand over Romeo's head, then dragged the guy toward the police. He didn't have time for detailed explanations. Laney needed to be found.

And the only person who knew where she was had been murdered.

"This man murdered Detective Kent Simmons using this weapon." He thrust the man and the gun toward the two officers. "There's a slug in the drywall of room five that you should be able to match to the gun. My daughter is still missing, I need to find her."

"Wait, you can't just leave," the officer protested.

Watch me, he thought. "Come, Romeo." He jogged back toward the White Horse Inn. As he grew closer, he saw Maggie arguing with a man outside the lobby.

"I need a key to every room here," she said. "My daughter's life is at stake!"

"Not without a warrant," the man insisted.

"Maggie, here. Let's try it this way." He joined her, then

once again pulled out Laney's clothing. "Seek! Seek Laney!"

Romeo eagerly stuck his nose into the clothing, then went to work. This time, Dallas stayed back, giving the dog room to explore.

The inn manager looked on with suspicious interest as Romeo sniffed all around the door to room five where Maggie and Simmons had been. Where Simmons's dead body still lay. Then the dog trotted down to the next room, and the next.

Dallas tried not to lose hope. If Laney wasn't here, then he wasn't sure where to go next.

Then Romeo pressed his nose to the bottom of the doorway of the last room in the row. Door number twelve. It was dark inside, but that didn't deter him.

Romeo turned, sat, and looked back at Dallas. His big, brown eyes seemed to say, "Hurry up!"

"Give me the key to room twelve or I'll break the door down," Dallas said to the manager. "You have two seconds to decide."

The man handed over what Dallas assumed was a master key. He and Maggie ran down to join Romeo. Dallas accessed the room and pushed the door open. Hitting the lights, he raked his gaze around the apparently empty room.

"Laney? Are you here?" he called sharply as Maggie joined him.

Thumping noises came from the bathroom. Romeo rushed forward, making whining sounds in his throat as he pawed at the door. Maggie wrenched it open, turned on the light, and gasped. "Laney! Are you all right?"

Laney's face was streaked with tears, a gag tied tightly around her mouth. Her arms and legs were bound too.

Maggie removed the gag first, then tried to undo the bindings.

"Let me." He pulled his MK 3 knife and sliced through the rope.

"Mommy," Laney cried, rubbing at her sore wrists and ankles. Then she threw herself into her mother's arms. "I knew you'd come. I knew you and Dad would come find me."

Tears of relief pricked his eyes, and he quickly blinked them away. "Romeo gets the credit," he managed. Had she really said, "Dad"?

"He does," Maggie agreed. She cradled Laney close. "We were so worried, Laney. How long were you in here?"

"I don't know." Laney sniffled and swiped at her face. "I thought he was safe. I knew he was your partner. He told me he was taking me home. But then . . . I don't know how, but I knew something was wrong."

"Romeo found your pink flip-flop." He eyed her with admiration. "You dropped it on purpose, didn't you?"

"Not exactly on purpose," Laney admitted sheepishly. "I struggled to get away, and it fell off. But I didn't say anything to Detective Simmons because I hoped Romeo would find it."

Hearing his name, the lab nuzzled Laney, licking her face and trying to crawl into her lap. Dallas realized he'd forgotten to reward the dog for his good work, but seeing the girl and dog wrapped together, he figured that finding Laney was reward enough.

Stupid tears pricked at his eyes again, and he had to take a step back to get his emotions under control.

Laney was safe. That was all that mattered.

"Daddy?" For a moment, he thought he was hearing things. Then he met Laney's gaze. "I'm glad you're here."

"Ah, Laney." He stepped into the tiny bathroom and bent toward her. To his surprise, she threw herself into his arms. Holding his daughter for the first time was incredible, and this time, the tears rolled unchecked down his cheeks.

His daughter. And her brave, smart, and beautiful mother.

His family.

"They're in here," a voice shouted. Seconds later, the sound of running feet.

Dallas wanted the police to go away, but he knew they wouldn't. After all, a man was dead, another had been disarmed after shooting him, and frankly, they still had a lot of explaining to do.

"I love you, Laney." He gave her one last hug, then loosened his grip. "We need to talk to the police, okay?"

"I love you too, Daddy." Laney stared up at him. "I'm sorry I ran away."

"It's okay, all that matters is that you're safe now." He met Maggie's gaze over Laney's head, then added, "Your mom was really worried, though. You shouldn't have put her through that."

"We were both worried," Maggie corrected. "But your dad is right. We're just happy you're safe. But the next time you're upset with us, because there will be a next time, I want you to talk to us rather than running away."

"I will," Laney promised.

"I see you found her," Detective Artes said from behind him.

Dallas turned to face him. "Romeo did." He wanted to lash out at the detective as they should have checked this place earlier, but he managed to hold his tongue. Alienating the police wouldn't help. And there hadn't been a black sedan either, so maybe it wasn't all their fault. The anger and frustration seeped away.

After Maggie called her mother to let her know they'd found Laney, they spent the next ninety minutes going through the events of the night.

Surprisingly, the FBI agents had arrived at the inn, sent by Sarah and accompanied by Tomlin, the ATF agent. They had possession of the original documents Tate had sent Maggie. After interrogating the suspect Dallas and Romeo had caught fleeing the scene, they were able to confirm Mitchell Werner was the man in charge who had ordered the killing of Simmons. Apparently, Werner felt the guy had outlived his usefulness as he hadn't come up with the documents Tate had sent to Maggie. From what they heard, the phone conversation between Maggie and Tate had been recorded, which is why Werner had sent gunmen after Maggie.

"We'll get a warrant, then go bust down Werner's door," Tomlin said with a grin. "Should be a fun night."

Dallas was too exhausted to care, but he had to admit that he'd once approached every op with the same enthusiasm. He admired Tomlin's persistence.

"Ready to go home?" he asked Maggie and Laney.

"Our house or the one with the pool?" Laney asked. There was a bit of lingering fear in her eyes that he knew would take time to fade.

"The one with the pool." His plan was to stay there until they knew Werner was no longer a threat. "We'll swim tomorrow, if that's okay with you."

Laney nodded, her subdued response tugging at his heart. She'd been through a terrible ordeal, and he wanted to take all her pain away.

Impossible, but still something he'd have given just about anything to accomplish.

"She'll be okay," Maggie murmured as they walked to the SUV.

"I know." He was carrying Laney because he didn't want her crossing the parking lot in her bare feet. Laney was relaxed against him as if drained of energy. His fingers brushed against Maggie's, and he caught her hand. "How are you? I'm sorry I took off, but I needed to get that guy. We need to take Mitchell Werner down to put this behind us."

"I know." Her smile was lopsided. "I'm okay. Let's get out of here."

He squeezed her hand, then opened the car door to put Laney in the back seat. Maggie crawled in beside her. He put Romeo in the back, glancing over when Detective Artes approached.

"We're going to have a cop stationed outside your place," Artes informed him. "Until we get the word from the ATF that the danger is over."

"Thanks, I appreciate that." He would take whatever additional protection they were willing to offer.

"We have you and your dog to thank for blowing the case open," Artes admitted. "Nice work."

Dallas nodded.

When they reached the house, he smiled when he saw Laney was leaning against Maggie, her eyes closed. "I'll carry her inside."

Laney stirred, then wrapped her arms around his neck. He carried her into the bedroom with Maggie beside him. She closed the window while he set Laney in her bed and patted the mattress. "Up, Romeo."

The lab eagerly jumped up to join Laney. His daughter

wrapped her arm around Romeo and snuggled in. "Good night, Mom. Good night, Dad."

"Good night, Laney." His heart nearly burst with love for the little girl.

Maggie's mom was waiting for them in the kitchen. "Are we safe now?"

Maggie glanced up at him, then nodded. "The feds are going after the person responsible. As soon as they find and arrest him, this nightmare will be over. Oh, and there's a cop posted outside too."

Sarah slowly nodded. "I'm glad to hear it. I guess the cookies will keep until tomorrow."

"Laney will love them," Maggie agreed.

"Good night." Sarah headed down to her room.

Once they were alone, he took Maggie's hand and drew her into the living room. "Let's talk for a minute."

To his surprise, she stiffened. "Not now, Dallas." She sighed, raking her hand through her hair. "I know you'll want some sort of co-custody arrangement with Laney, but I just can't deal with that tonight."

"That wasn't what I wanted to talk about at all," he protested. "I won't lie to you, of course I want time with Laney, but this is about us, Maggie. About you and me."

She eyed him warily. "Okay." It was more question than agreement.

He wasn't eloquent by nature. "When I realized you were in danger, I nearly lost my mind. I was so worried about you." When she opened her mouth, he held up a hand. "Yes, I know you're a trained cop, and I trust your skills. But the truth is, I was beside myself over the possibility of losing you."

"That's sweet, Dallas. And I will admit your crash

entrance into the motel room was a very welcome distraction."

"Like I said, I know you're a well-trained cop. And I know God was watching over us, but my biggest regret was not telling you how I feel." He took both of her hands in his. "I love you, Maggie. I loved you nine years ago, and in the years since, I've never let another woman get close. Being with you now only makes me realize how much I still love you."

He felt her fingers tremble within his, but her gaze was steady. "Are you sure this isn't about having Laney full time? After all, if we get together, you won't have to settle for co-custody."

"It's not about Laney at all." He felt his temper slip. "Maggie, I have never loved anyone the way I loved you. And yes, we are different people now, but these past few days have only shown me that you're a better, stronger woman than the one I left behind. I hope you can agree that I've changed too. Hopefully for the better."

She nodded, her deep brown eyes searching his as if trying to read his thoughts. "I made a mistake marrying Tate. I don't want to make another one."

A smile tugged at the corner of his mouth. He hadn't asked her to marry him, but he liked that she was thinking about it. "I would never force you into something you're not ready for. All I'm asking is that you give me a chance. Give *us* a chance. We didn't have that opportunity nine years ago, but I'd like to think we could try again."

"But if things don't work out, Laney will get hurt."

"Not just Laney. We'll both be hurting if things don't work out. But going into a relationship with doubts isn't the way to approach this." He hesitated, then added, "I guess I'm asking if you have any feelings for me at all."

"Oh, Dallas." She sighed, pulled her hands free, and reached out to hug him. "Yes, I have feelings. I love you too. I didn't want to, but I do."

It was a backhanded compliment, but he decided to take it. "Good. Let's start with that and work forward from there, okay?"

"Okay." She smiled up at him, and heaven help him, he couldn't help but capture her mouth with his.

Maggie melted against him, kissing him back with all the passion they'd once shared. The years melted away, and he knew Maggie Chandler had always possessed his heart.

He gave it to her nine years ago, and he didn't mind her having it now.

They kissed for a long time, but he soon lifted his head and tucked her in close. "I almost lost you tonight," he murmured. "You and Laney are the two most important people in my life."

"As you said, God was watching over us." She rested her hand on his chest. "I love you, Dallas. I always have."

"I love you too." He pressed a kiss to her temple, thinking of the difficulties they'd both endured over the past nine years. Tough times, but every minute of every day was well worth it to end up here. Holding Maggie in his arms.

Together at last.

EPILOGUE

Two weeks later . . .

Maggie looked around the house she shared with her mother realizing it would be too small for all of them to live there together.

Not that Dallas had mentioned living together. Or getting married.

Her fault because she'd insisted on taking things slow. Because of Laney, who still woke up crying from nightmares from her kidnapping. Having Romeo sleep with her each night helped, and the nightmares were finally getting less frequent.

Agent Tomlin had raided Mitchell Werner's home the same night they'd rescued Laney, finding more than enough evidence to put the guy away, but he hadn't been there. A week later, they'd found Werner trying to cross the border into Mexico. He was now being held in a federal prison without bail while awaiting trial.

The moment the news had reached them, they'd returned to Fredericksburg. Dallas rented the house across the street temporarily, which had been rented by one of

Werner's guys to watch Maggie's place. It was nice having him nearby, but she knew they'd have to make some sort of permanent plans soon.

Preferably before Laney started school.

"Mags?" Dallas walked into the living area. Romeo was at his side, but in his arms he held an adorable yellow lab puppy.

"You didn't," she said, a reluctant smile creasing her features.

"Oh great," her mother said with a sigh. But a smile tugged at the corner of her mouth. Maggie knew her mother had come to love Romeo, especially after he'd found Laney.

Dallas grinned. "Meet Juliet." He glanced toward her mother. "Come on, Sarah. You're not really going to argue about Romeo needing some companionship, are you?"

At the sound of his name, Romeo whined, his tail wagging furiously. Clearly, he already loved the new addition to the family.

Her mother reluctantly smiled. "I guess not."

Maggie rolled her eyes. "I'm not buying that story. You bought that puppy for Laney, didn't you?"

"Juliet will be part of the family," he said evasively. "Now check her collar."

Her heart melted as the puppy nuzzled close. "She's adorable, but you know she belongs to Laney."

"Check the collar," he repeated.

Shifting the dog to one arm, she gently fingered the collar. There was a ring hanging from it. Her heart thudded painfully against her chest as she realized it was a diamond ring.

An engagement ring?

"I—don't understand." She stared at him.

"Maggie Chandler, will you please do me the honor of

becoming my wife?" He grinned and lightly stroked Juliet's fur while holding her gaze. "The puppy is for Laney, but that's only because I wanted to give our daughter something special too. I love you both very much."

An engagement ring for her and a puppy for their daughter. Dallas had been nothing but a gentleman these past two weeks, which she both appreciated and fretted over. Yet his kisses held the same passion and promise they always had.

"Please, Mags. Please marry me." He looked uncertain now, as if she might refuse him. He glanced over to where her mother was watching them, her eyes bright with tears.

"Yes, Dallas. I would love to marry you." The words didn't cause even the vaguest twinge of regret. Nothing like the ball of dread that had sat in her stomach during her first marriage. "And I know Laney will love Juliet too."

"Mags, you've made me the happiest man in the world." He pulled her into his arms, but the dog wiggled so much they barely had time to kiss.

"I'm thrilled for both of you," her mom said. "And I'll say this, it's about time."

"Thanks, Mom. You're welcome to stay with us too." She didn't want her mother to feel left out. "We need your help with Laney."

"And the dogs," her mother replied dryly.

Maggie couldn't argue because it was true. "Thanks, Mom."

"That reminds me, this is for you." Dallas crossed over to hand her mother a small jewelry box.

"Me?" Her mother looked uncertain. She opened the box and gasped. She carefully lifted the heart pendant from the cotton. "Oh, Dallas, it's beautiful."

Maggie's heart melted. Trust Dallas to provide all three of them with gifts.

"Hey, is that a puppy?" Laney came into the house, her eyes wide with glee as she noticed the yellow lab. She'd been swimming at her friend Jane's house and was still wearing her swimsuit.

Dallas winked at Maggie, then gently took the puppy, and crossed over to Laney. "This is Juliet. She's yours, but I want you to look at her collar."

"Oh, love her," Laney gushed. "She's really mine?"

"That means you have to take care of her," Maggie warned.

"I will!"

Dallas sighed. "Look at her collar."

Laney laughed when Juliet licked her chin, but then her eyes widened in surprise when she saw the ring attached to the puppy's collar. Laney gaped at her parents. "Does this mean?"

"Yes, your mom and I are getting married," Dallas said. "I hope you're okay with that."

"I knew it!" Laney jumped and danced with the puppy in her arms. Romeo eagerly danced around the room with her. "I knew you two would get married. Yay! I'm so happy for you. And for me!"

Maggie laughed and shook her head. "Well then, I guess that's settled."

"I think we should stay here in Fredericksburg," Dallas said. "But we need a bigger house with a pool."

Lieutenant Fernando had brought her back to work the moment Mitchell Werner was arrested. She was the senior detective now, and they were trying to hire someone to replace Kent Simmons. His turning dirty had put a pall over the entire police force, but Fernando was doing his best to overcome the negative press. "Okay, we can start looking for a new house."

"I also applied to become a cop with the Fredericksburg Police Department." Dallas shrugged. "My therapist gave me the okay to push my shoulder a bit. I think I can pass the physical."

"You don't have to do that," she protested.

"Yes, I do." He smiled. "Retirement isn't my thing. I either become a cop or a private investigator. To be honest, I think a cop is more my style."

She and Tate had been cops together on the force, which hadn't always worked out well. But having Dallas as a member of the team didn't bother her at all.

"I think you're right. You'll be a great cop, Dallas." She laughed when Laney rushed the puppy outside before she could squat to pee. Romeo bounded after them, and her mother went out too, giving Laney instructions on how to train the new puppy. Maggie chuckled. "I can guarantee our lives will never be boring."

"I'm counting on that." Dallas swept her into his arms for a deep kiss. "Especially if we add a brother or sister for Laney."

The idea made her head spin, but in a good way. "I love you, Dallas."

"I love you too." Arms wrapped around each other, they watched as their daughter played with Romeo and Juliet beneath her nana's watchful eyes.

This was her family.

I HOPE you enjoyed Dallas and Maggie's story in *Sealed with Trust*. Are you ready to wrap up the series with Nico and Ava's story in *Sealed with Valor*? Click here!

DEAR READER

Dear Reader,

I hope you are enjoying my Called to Protect series. I'm having fun writing about these Navy SEAL heroes who are struggling with the pain of losing a teammate while trying to adapt to civilian life. The least I could do was help them find love. I hope you enjoyed Dallas and Maggie's story.

I'm hard at work finishing up Nico and Ava's story in *Sealed with Valor*. I hope you enjoy the last book in this series.

I adore hearing from my readers! I can be found through my website at https://www.laurascottbooks.com, via Facebook at https://www.facebook.com/ LauraScottBooks, Instagram at https://www.instagram. com/laurascottbooks/, and Twitter https://twitter.com/ laurascottbooks. Also, take a moment to sign up for my monthly newsletter, all subscribers receive a free novella, *Starting Over*, that is not available for purchase on any platform.

Until next time,

Laura Scott

PS: If you're interested in a sneak peek of *Sealed with Valor*, I've included the first chapter here.

SEALED WITH VALOR

Former Navy SEAL Nico Ramirez was stretched out on a hill overlooking a dilapidated apartment building with his Doberman, Zulu, lying beside him. This was his first solid lead in the seven months he'd been trying to find his swim buddy's younger sister, Ava. Jaydon Rampart hadn't survived their last mission, the one that had sidelined him for weeks after rupturing his Achilles tendon. Losing Jaydon had been tough, but if that wasn't bad enough, when he'd gone to see Ava after Jaydon's memorial service, he'd discovered she was missing.

At first, he'd thought she'd simply needed time and space to grieve her brother. He'd been healing from his own surgery too. But after one week became two, the warning bells in the back of his mind had gone off.

He'd followed one lead after another. He'd discovered Ava had spent time at a Los Angeles battered women's shelter back in March, but then had disappeared without telling anyone where she was going. Her boyfriend, Simon Marks, AKA Simon Normandy, was the one who'd caused her to seek shelter in the first place, according Charlotte, the woman who ran the shelter. And that made him more determined to find her.

But every clue he'd followed up on had led to a dead end. He was beyond frustrated, yet he had refused to give up.

Would never give up. Not until he found her.

Finally, after what seemed like eons, Ava's friend Jill had heard from her. From what Jill had explained, Ava had been crying, saying something about needing to hear a friendly voice. Jill had tried to soothe her friend, to assure her that everything would be okay. But when Jill had pressed for details as to where she was, Ava had quickly said she had to go and disconnected from the call.

It had taken Nico several days and calling in a big favor from Bryce O'Malley, one of his law enforcement buddies, to trace Ava's call. Which had led him here to San Bernardino, California.

And to this sketchy-looking apartment building.

He peered again through the binoculars. He'd been hoping to catch a glimpse of Ava going in or coming out of the building, but so far, he hadn't seen her. Or anyone looking like her. He was certain Ava had changed her appearance in the months she'd been gone. But she couldn't change her skin color, and most of the people going in and out of the building had either been white men or men and women of color.

The sun dipped low on the horizon as the hour headed toward seven o'clock in the evening. Early September and the days were already growing short. Nico had been here for several hours, leaving only to take care of his K9 partner, Zulu.

Zulu was a high-energy Doberman that he'd gotten back when he and the other guys had met with Lillian, the woman who rescued dogs and helped train them for military vets. Mason Grey, their senior chief, had arranged for every one of them to get a dog. The moment he'd set eyes on the female Doberman, Nico had known she was for him.

He watched for a few more minutes and was about to lower his binocs to give Zulu a break when he froze. A woman was walking toward the apartment building, crossing the street in front of him. He could only see her from the back, but she was white with short and curly blond hair. She wore a casual yellow sundress and sandals in deference to the heat.

Ava had always worn her red hair long and straight, but that didn't mean much. He could also count on one hand how many times he'd seen her wearing a dress, she'd always lived in jeans and other casual clothes, but again, things could have changed. He slowly turned the binocs to get a closer look at her profile.

His heart thudded against his rib cage as he watched her striding toward the door. "Come on," he whispered under his breath. "Show me your face."

As if on cue, the woman turned to glance furtively behind her as if concerned she was being followed. Nico almost dropped his binocs when he saw Ava's familiar beautiful features etched in fear.

He'd found her! He surged to his feet. "Come, Zulu!" The apartment building wasn't secure, but he wanted to catch Ava before she disappeared into one of the apartments. He'd already checked the names on the mailboxes, but there was no Ava Rampart.

No surprise since she'd likely changed her name to match her altered appearance.

He ran down the hill and across the street with Zulu at his side. His ruptured Achilles tendon was healed now, but it still gave him a twinge when he did things like move abruptly. Ignoring the pain, he managed to catch up to Ava just as she was crossing the threshold going inside the apartment building.

Sensing his presence, she began to run, but he grabbed her arm. "Ava, it's me. Nico."

She spun to face him, her mouth dropping in surprise. "N-Nico? How did you find me?"

"I've been searching for you since March." Nico's gaze dropped to her belly. Her very pregnant belly. For a moment, he couldn't move, couldn't even think. The baby had to be Simon's, which only made him more angry at how the guy had physically abused her. Somehow, he managed to find his voice. "Let's go. I know you're in trouble, and I'm here to help."

She shook her head and grabbed his arm. "Come inside. We can't talk here."

Zulu growled, which caused Ava to drop his arm and step back in fear. He put a hand on Zulu and reached out to take Ava's hand. "Friend, Zulu. Ava is a friend."

"Renee," she hissed. "I'm Renee."

"Friend, Zulu," he dutifully repeated. "Renee is a friend."

Zulu wagged her butt, her tail having been cropped before Lillian had been able to prevent it, and licked Ava, er —Renee's hand. Satisfied she wasn't going to be bitten, Ava opened the door and led the way inside.

Nico remembered seeing a Renee on the mailbox for apartment number 3. Ava pulled out her key and unlocked the door, one that would buckle under a well-placed kick, he thought grimly. He kept his thoughts to himself as she gestured for him to come inside.

The place was surprisingly clean, despite the roach

traps set in every corner of the place. He swallowed hard, hating the way Ava had been forced to live like this. She closed and locked the door. Then tucked her keys back in her oversized purse that she wore crossways over her body.

In a way, that only magnified her pregnancy.

"I need to know how you found me." She walked over and sank down onto the sofa, wincing as if her feet were killing her. "Because if you found me, Simon will too."

"You've been running from him all this time?" He heard his voice rising in anger and tried to dial it back a notch. "If you would have just reached out to me, you wouldn't be stuck in a place like this. Better yet, why didn't you go to the police?"

She narrowed her eyes. "First of all, I didn't know you were looking for me. Secondly, you don't seem to understand the seriousness of the situation. I can't go to the police, there are—reasons. They don't matter right now, all that I care about is flying under the radar. Every time I think I'm safe, one of Simon's goons find me." Her hand rested on her belly. "I need to know, Nico. How did you find me?"

"I traced your call to Jill." He came over to sit beside her. "You're not alone anymore, Ava. I'm here, and I'll keep you safe from Simon. But I need to understand why you can't go to the police."

"Jill?" Her eyes widened as in horror at her mistake. She stood with a grimace. "I need to get out of here."

"I'll take care of you," he repeated. "Do you need to pack anything? Um, you know, for your baby?"

She arched a brow. "I don't have anything for the baby yet, I'm not due until late November. I would like to grab some clothes. It's not easy to find maternity clothes on the run. Oh, and I need to get Callie too."

"Callie? Who's that?"

Ava didn't answer, disappearing into the bedroom. He paced the small apartment, his mind whirling. Ava was having a baby by the end of November.

Simon's baby.

No, her baby. Simon didn't deserve to have his name associated with an innocent child. Just the thought of him striking at Ava while she was pregnant made his gaze go red with fury. And what was this about not being able to go to the cops? His gut tightened. He didn't understand, but he would learn everything very soon.

But this wasn't the time or the place to grill her about Simon. If she was right about Simon and his goons finding her, they needed to get out of Dodge.

Or in this case, out of San Bernardino.

"I'm ready." Ava stopped in the small kitchen area to grab a bottle of what looked like vitamins. She stuffed them into the backpack she held in one hand.

"I'll take that." He reached for the pack and slung it over his shoulder. "Who is Callie?"

"She's a friend. One I've been trying to keep safe too." Ava avoided his gaze as she headed for the door. "She'll be at work, so we'll need to pick her up on the way."

"Come, Zulu." His K9 stayed at his side as he quickly caught up to Ava. He held his Sig Sauer pistol in his hand. "Let me go first. I want you to stay behind me."

For the first time, she seemed to soften. "Thank you, Nico."

"Always." There was so much more he wanted to say, but his questions and concerns would have to wait. Once they were in the hall, he stopped her with a hand on her arm. "Is there a back door?"

"Good point. This way." She gestured down the hall, in

the opposite direction of the front door. He nodded, taking the lead with Zulu beside him.

At the back door to the building, he took a moment to rake his gaze over the area. Seeing nothing alarming, he pushed the door open and stepped out. "Stay close," he told Ava. "I left my SUV a few blocks down the road."

If he'd have known about her pregnancy, he'd have parked closer. For a nanosecond, he considered having her stay here so he could fetch the car so she wouldn't have to walk on her sore feet. But now that he'd found her, he wasn't about to let her out of his sight.

Ava didn't complain as they made their way along the back of the building. Upon reaching the corner, he paused to peer around it.

A movement caught his eye. A man was lurking near the building next door. He narrowed his gaze, then turned to Ava. He put his mouth to her ear. "Is that Simon or one of his thugs?"

He moved just enough so she could see the man for herself. She stared for a long moment, then shook her head. "I don't recognize him. But that doesn't mean Simon didn't switch things up."

Great. Nico privately thought the guy was suspicious enough to avoid drawing the lurker's attention. Several people hanging out was normal, but this? Not so much.

"Let's go the other way." He turned and hugged the back of the building to the other corner. It was the opposite direction from where he'd left his Jeep, but it couldn't be helped. When he reached that corner, he took another peek.

There was no one around. Breathing a sigh of relief, he led the way to the next building, and the next, until he found one where they could head around the block to where his Jeep was waiting.

Zulu was a dark shadow at his side, and he was grateful for her presence. Ava was breathing heavily by the time they arrived at his Jeep. A flash of concern hit hard. He had zero knowledge of pregnant women, but running around couldn't be good for her or the baby.

"Are you okay?" he asked. He holstered his weapon and opened the passenger door for her to get inside.

"I'm fine." Her curt tone didn't invite comment.

When she was settled, he closed the door and took Zulu around to the back hatch. The moment he opened it, Zulu jumped inside, knowing what was expected of her. Slamming the hatch shut, he quickly went to the driver's side to get behind the wheel. "Ready? I want us to get far away from that guy lurking near your apartment building. We need to get out of the city."

"I agree, but after we pick up Callie." She struggled to get the seat belt around her belly. "I'm not leaving her, Nico, so don't bother arguing with me."

He ground his back molars together as he pulled away from the curb. Every instinct made him want to drive far away without looking back. "Okay, where is she?"

"She's a waitress at the Lizard Lounge. It's only a few blocks from here."

He remembered passing the place on his way to the apartment building. "Do you work there too?"

"Yes." She didn't elaborate, but it explained why her feet were sore. He hated thinking about her standing and serving people all day but told himself to let it go. Now that he'd found her, he planned to keep her safe. And off her feet at least until she had the baby.

Once they were settled, he'd call the rest of his team to let them know he'd found Ava. All six members of the SEAL team had been concerned about her disappearance.

His five teammates had tried to help him in various ways despite suffering their own injuries sustained in their last op. Some of them, like Hudd, had been injured worse than others.

And weirdly, they'd all fallen in love over the past seven months. Once he'd imagined himself in love with Ava, but that had been years ago when she'd been too young for the likes of him.

Now she was pregnant and in danger. A romantic relationship was out of the question. Which was fine. That wasn't why he'd come for her. He'd known Jaydon, his swim buddy all through BUD/S training, would expect him to find his sister and keep her safe.

After long months, he finally had found her. He sent up a silent prayer, asking for God's grace and strength to enable him to keep Ava and her unborn child safe from harm.

AVA TWISTED her fingers in her lap, doing her best to ignore Nico's overwhelming presence beside her.

Shocking to learn he'd been looking for her all this time. She was grateful for his reassuring presence but couldn't help feeling on edge.

Simon was out there, looking for her with the intent to silence her once and for all. Callie, too, which is why she needed to get to the woman she viewed as a sister.

Because they both knew too much.

She and Callie had been moving from city to city, managing to stay one step ahead of Simon and his goons. She knew Nico would badger her about going to the police, but he didn't understand what she'd done. Only out of necessity, but that wasn't how it would look. No, she couldn't risk having her baby in jail, so she'd done everything possible to stay off Simon's radar. Her goal, and Callie's too, was to stay hidden until she had the baby.

After that, their plan was to head to Mexico, disappearing forever.

Now that Nico Ramirez had found her, she knew her plan was in jeopardy. Nico would keep looking for her, no matter what. And staying to fight wasn't an option. What could one man do against Simon's empire?

Not much. And she had to swallow a ball of fear that Nico would only get hurt too.

The way Brent Green had when he'd tried to help four months ago.

Her stomach clenched at the thought of having more blood on her hands. She wouldn't be able to live with herself if Nico died in a vain effort to save her too.

So much death and destruction, and for what? Money. It all came down to cold, hard cash.

"Wait! Where are you going?" she asked sharply. Nico had turned on the next street, heading several blocks away from the Lizard Lounge. She twisted in her seat, no easy feat, to check out the back window. "Is someone following us?"

"No, you're safe." He glanced at her, his dark brown eyes shimmering with concern. "You need to trust me, Ava. I'm not going to let anything happen to you."

She wanted to trust him, but after so many months being on the run and in hiding, she couldn't seem to drop her guard. Especially since Nico really had no idea who he was up against. Sure, he was a Navy SEAL the way her brother once was, before Jaydon had been killed by an underwater bomb explosion. But he was still only one man up against a ruthless killer. Her fingers knotted as he went several blocks out of the way before finally turning around at the next block to head back toward the Lizard Lounge.

He pulled into the parking lot, then backed into a spot near the exit. Keeping the car running, he turned toward her. "What does Callie look like? I'll go inside to get her."

She rolled her eyes. "Callie isn't going to go anywhere with you, a complete stranger. She'll assume you were sent by Simon too. I'll get her."

"No way am I letting you head inside alone." His curt tone irritated her. Partially because she was tired and crabby after being on her feet for eight hours. Her job was to bartend, while Callie worked as a waitress. It wasn't a bad job, and she did well with tips. At least, she had before she'd become so noticeably pregnant.

"One look at you, and she'll run." Ava reached over to lightly touch his arm. His skin was so hot it was a wonder her fingertips didn't blister from the heat. "I'll need to reassure her that you're not with Simon. Just give me a few minutes to talk to her, okay?"

"Fine. We'll go in together," he said with obvious reluctance.

She stared at him for a long moment, then sighed. "Fine. But you need to let me take the lead. I don't need you scaring Callie to death. We've only been here in San Bernardino for the past four weeks. We just moved into that apartment." And deep down, she was mad that she had to leave, all because of a moment of weakness.

Why had she contacted Jill? She knew better than to do something so stupid. But her hormones were running amuck, and she'd had a breakdown after a particularly brutal day at work.

She'd never realized how being isolated from everyone you knew could wear a person down.

Enough. She'd told herself there was no point in wallowing in self-pity. This mess was her fault for falling for Simon in the first place. Not that she ever could have anticipated being on the run for her life when she'd started seeing him.

That she'd be forced to kill another human being in order to escape.

A wave of nausea hit hard. She ruthlessly shoved the memory aside. Time to move forward. They couldn't stick around San Bernardino for long. She slid out of the passenger seat with all the grace of a baby buffalo, wincing as she stood on her sore and swollen feet. She managed to shut the door behind her and moved toward the front of the restaurant. Nico quickly joined her, slipping his hand beneath her elbow.

"What about Zulu?"

"I left the windows down for her. And I can remotely start the Jeep with the air-conditioning on full blast, if this takes longer than it should."

She nodded, impressed with how much he cared for his dog. After her initial fear of the Doberman had faded, she'd realized Nico and Zulu were quite a dynamic pair. And the way Zulu had licked her hand when Nico introduced her had been sweet.

Casting a quick glance around the parking lot, she hurried up to the door. Nico kept pace behind her, reaching around to open the door when she arrived.

A weak blast of air-conditioning hit when she crossed the threshold. She stood there for a moment, searching for Callie. The girl had dark hair that had been resistant to hair dye, making it harder for her to escape Simon's notice. Callie had cut it short, but even that didn't alter her appearance much.

"How come you weren't wearing one of those uniforms?" Nico asked in a low voice.

"I was, but I changed." The uniform he mentioned was a white, off-the-shoulder peasant blouse with a brightly colored skirt. Even the female bartenders were forced to wear them, which seemed silly to her. But it was a job, and Pedro, the boss, hadn't asked many questions other than how soon she and Callie could start working.

Their answer? Immediately.

"Where is she?" Nico asked, his tone laced with impatience. "We need to get out of here."

"I don't see her." Which was strange as the tables were more than half full. Normally, Callie would be hustling back and forth, chatting with her customers. Her friend was a great waitress. Better than she was a bartender, that was for sure.

Ava wove through the tables, taking care not to bump into anyone as she went. When she reached the corner of the bar, she waited to catch Ramon's eye. "Where's Callie?"

"No idea." Ramon was barely twenty-one and treated her like she was eighty rather than thirty-two. "I think Pedro is looking for her too."

A chill snaked down her spine. Why would Pedro be looking for her? Callie's shift didn't end for another hour yet.

"Come on, we need to hurry," Nico said.

"I'm trying," she snapped. Then she took a deep breath. He was probably worried about Zulu being in the car. Thankfully, the sun was down, but still, the heat could still be oppressive. She headed around the bar toward the back room where Pedro, the owner and manager, had a tiny office, when he came rushing toward her.

"Renee! Where is Callie?" He was short, his dark hair liberally laced with gray. "Did she go home with you?"

The chill coalesced to ice. "No. She's not with me. How long as she been gone?" She glanced back at Nico. He'd taken an alternate route, so they wouldn't have passed Callie along the way.

"Ten or fifteen minutes," Pedro said. "She took her break but didn't come back. I thought maybe she went to see you." Pedro flushed, glancing at her stomach. "I tell myself the baby might have come early."

"I'm fine, and I haven't seen her." She pushed past Pedro to check the small break area for herself.

The small round table tucked into the corner of the supply room was empty.

She swallowed hard and turned to face Nico. "Callie wouldn't take off like this, not without a good reason. She's a good worker."

"You think Simon's men found her?" Nico asked, his expression grave.

She closed her eyes, leaned against him, and nodded. And the worst part was that if Simon had Callie, he wouldn't hesitate to use her as bait to get to her.

And their unborn child.

34589180R00139